JD

by Evan Jacobs

Ronni's Books/Anhedenia Films

Artwork by C.J. Duke

Edited by Alex Faber

Layout by Mike Hartsfield

For Morris Fisher and the kids who continue to help me help them

And for Shawn Miller... a great person and friend

Chapter 1.

RJ Boynton walked up to the bowling alley knowing two things: he was mad and he was gonna beat up Tim Craig because of it.

"You can't do this," Yogi Jamison said with a slight lisp. He had mostly stopped doing it, but RJ found that Yogi lisped more when he was scared.

"Why not?" RJ asked, more distracted than annoyed by the question.

"Because you can't. Tim's brother works at the bowling alley. So do all his brother's friends. If you beat him up his brothers are gonna pound you."

"They'll have to catch me first," RJ stated. He was starting to feel that excited fight feeling he got as soon as he turned the corner and saw the Lincoln Lanes Bowling Alley.

"I hope Yogi can keep up," RJ thought as they moved closer to it.

He was planning on being really quick against Tim Craig. One minute Tim would be standing there playing a video game or something; the next he would be getting punched and kicked, and then after that he'd be on the ground.

"This was how it was going to be," RJ told himself. "This was how it had to be."

Earlier that day Tim had made a comment about RJ's Mom. He probably regretted it after he said it. He definitely did after RJ scowled and then smiled at him. It was RJ's way of telling Tim, "We're in school right now but we won't be forever." It all went back to something RJ's big brother Joel taught him:

"Never get someone when they expect you to."

2.

    The arcade was pretty busy that Friday afternoon. RJ moved past people swiftly since only he and Yogi knew what he was going to do, and since Yogi wasn't really going to do anything he didn't really count.
    RJ felt invisible. And that was just the way he liked it.
    He stopped walking suddenly. In the food area, RJ saw Tim Craig eating with someone who was probably his dad. "They look so normal," RJ thought. But Tim's dad had no idea about the awful thing his son had said about RJ's mom. He had no idea how much his son made fun of RJ for being in the "stupid classes," for not having money like them, for not having... anything Tim had.
    "He might know all this later," RJ wondered for a moment. That was if Tim admitted it... if he admitted why RJ kicked his butt.
    "Let's go, he's with his dad. You'll get in trouble for sure." Yogi pleaded.
    Yogi was more nervous today than usual. It was probably because Lincoln Lanes was so far from their house. It might be a long getaway. RJ's eyes darted around the bowling alley to try and see if he could spot Mike or Larry: Tim Craig's older brothers. So far he hadn't.
    "No," RJ stated. Tim's dad being there complicated things but RJ would just lay low, bide his time and wait until he got Tim alone. Then he'd really get him. RJ had done this so many times before, he felt like he was prepared for anything that might happen.

    Yogi was getting tired of the bowling alley. The constant sounds of the balls smashing into pins, the noises from the video games, people's voices, etc. Normally these things didn't bother him that much, but he was more on edge than normal. He regretted not having a snack now but he hadn't anticipated

RJ coming over. When he did, Yogi was quick to keep him out of sight of his parents because they didn't like RJ. They thought he was a bad influence. Usually, Yogi and RJ just hung out in his room or quickly went outside. Like today.

    RJ glared at Tim, who was still eating with his dad. They were just eating fries and drinking Cokes but they were taking forever doing it.

    "What could they be talking about for so long?" RJ asked himself. "If my dad was here... if Joel was here, we'd both take them on."

    But RJ's dad wasn't there. He never would be. RJ's father was dead. He died when RJ was five. Rick Boynton had had a drug and alcohol problem. He was also involved with some really "shady" people. According to his mom, RJ's dad had gone out one night and never come back. A month later the police found his body in a dumpy hotel room in Arizona.

    RJ's brother Joel was in jail for drugs now. He had been living in Colorado before coming back to California. He'd gotten busted and was sent to Rittner Jail (which was two hours away) for eight months. When he got out, he promised RJ that he'd come see him. RJ hoped he'd stay with him and his mom. Or, maybe he could go with Joel if he was gonna stay somewhere else? It was gonna be great when his brother came back to town. Yogi was RJ's best friend but he wasn't nearly as much fun as Joel. RJ loved his mom but he had so many questions about things, things his mom didn't seem to have the time to tell him. Things he would feel weird talking to her about.

    RJ's thoughts were interrupted as Tim and his father started to leave the table. Tim got up first and walked away from his dad. He seemed headed for the bathroom. After that he was probably going to meet his dad at the lane they were using, or at the front of the bowling alley if they were leaving. Chances were one of Tim's brothers was working. RJ had been surprised that they hadn't seen him yet. Joel had taught RJ that before he jumped someone he should take in everything going on around him. To absorb it and then figure out the simplest way to do what needed to be done.

"It's something you should do for everything. Whether you're boosting a car or getting in a fight, if you know your surroundings you can make anything happen."

"I'm gonna get him in the bathroom." RJ said as he moved away from Yogi.

"What?!? You can't..." Yogi started to say, but RJ was gone. Now Yogi really wished that he'd stayed home.

RJ walked slowly into the bathroom. He stopped when he saw Tim at a urinal and took note of someone else being in one of the stalls. It wasn't his dad because RJ didn't see him go into the bathroom. RJ waited behind the hallway wall that led into the bathroom. The sounds of the bowling alley were lower in there but they could still be heard. The urinal flushed and RJ's heart started to beat faster.

"This is gonna be so good," he told himself. "All the kids will be talking about it on Monday."

Tim went to wash his hands, but RJ's real cue came when he heard him pull the paper towel.

"What's up?" RJ asked loudly as he walked around the corner of the bathroom hallway. He felt the excitement starting to grow within him as he saw how scared Tim was. RJ moved closer and pushed him against the wall.

"Cut it out, RJ! You're gonna get in big trouble!"

"What'd you say about my mom?" He knew what Tim had said. RJ was just savoring every moment of this ritual.

"I don't know?!?" Tim's fear was doing nothing but feeding RJ's anger.

RJ hit Tim in the face. It wasn't that hard but it wasn't supposed to be. RJ wanted to toy with Tim Craig. Make him think this beating wasn't going to be that bad. This was another thing Joel had taught him.

"You don't know??? You don't remember making fun of my mom because she's sick?!?!"

RJ started to unload on Tim with more punches and kicks than he had ever thrown in his life. The first punch he landed on the top of Tim's head had sent a very sharp pain up RJ's entire arm, but he wasn't about to let that stop him. He continued to punch Tim's head, his shoulders, his arms, etc. As Tim started to fall down, RJ began to kick him as hard as he could. Sometimes he'd miss and kick the wall but that didn't stop him at all. When RJ got in a fight everything went black and he just fought on instinct. He always remembered another one of Joel's rules about fighting:

"If you're gonna hit someone, hit them until they can't get up anymore."

Tim lay on the ground trying to curl up into a ball so he could block the blows. He was crying now. RJ had thought that this might be enough, but he had so much energy, he was so angry, he couldn't stop. He'd been so involved he hadn't even heard how loud Tim was screaming.

Suddenly, two large hands picked RJ up and threw him across the other side of the bathroom.

"What are you doing?!?!" a man asked in an angry voice. He had seemed to magically appear and RJ was still trying to process everything. The man wore a blue tank top and faded blue jeans. RJ was quick to realize that this wasn't Tim's dad. Whoever it was, he was too old to be his brother. "What's the matter with you?!?"

All RJ wanted to do now was get out of the bowling alley. He hadn't beaten Tim up as badly as he wanted, but he'd done pretty good. Joel would've been proud.

The man reached for RJ. RJ pulled the bathroom door open and ran right past Tim's dad. It was as if the moment he saw RJ, he knew the noises that he had heard in the bathroom involved his son. RJ had had problems with Tim and his family before, but nothing like this. RJ kept running. All he had to do was make it down this long stretch of lanes, turn right, and he could run out the glass doors.

Yogi was standing by a wall near the opening of the bowling alley. He watched RJ run up.

"What happened?!?!"

"LET'S GO!" RJ yelled.

Right then he saw Tim's brother, Mike, turn his head. He was working the front counter now. He had kicked RJ out of Lincoln Lanes a bunch of times. He had never liked him and as soon as he saw RJ running in the bowling alley (which was against the rules), he was immediately suspicious.

"HEY!" Mike barked.

RJ kept running. He was home free as he turned right toward the sliding glass door entrance. Then, for a split second, he looked back to see if Yogi was with him. RJ must've been going so fast that he didn't see the sign that the sliding doors were being serviced and customers should use the manual ones. He and Yogi had gone in the side doors of the bowling alley today to avoid being seen coming through the front.

All of this came crashing down on RJ as he ran through the closed sliding glass doors, shattering them as he toppled down the concrete steps outside.

Chapter 2.

Yogi went home shortly after the police took RJ to the hospital. He was scratched up on his face and neck, and he'd broken his arm hitting Tim Craig on top of the head. He didn't know what would bother his Mom more: the sight of her son's Band-Aids or the big, white, pristine cast that now covered most of his arm. She would probably be the most upset about him fighting again, and then there was the little matter of the hospital bill... not to mention the damage RJ had caused by shattering the glass door at Lincoln Lanes.

Right now, none of this concerned RJ. Even with two police officers waiting with him, all he could think about was what a great story this was going to be at school on Monday. Some of the scratches might actually look cool, especially when they scabbed over. He thought he might tell people that he got in a fight with Wolverine from the X-Men movies.

RJ had always been the person that other kids didn't want to fight, but now they really wouldn't mess with him. "And none of them will ever think about making fun of my mom again," he thought.

It seemed like the moment he had that thought his mom appeared in the hospital discharge area. She always looked tired to RJ. She hadn't always been like that. RJ remembered when he was a little bit younger she had had a lot more energy. She used to go out with her friends (even after his dad died) but she didn't do much of anything anymore. She worked two jobs. She slept a lot and barely got out of her pajamas when she was off. Some mornings she would make RJ lunch, but most of the time he got a free one from the school (breakfast too). Due to her medication, she seemed out of it when he spoke to her. It was probably a huge effort for her to leave work and come down to the hospital to get him.

RJ loved his mom. She let him do what he wanted as long as he worked on his homework one hour a day after school. Oftentimes, if she was home, he'd take his backpack, go into his room, shut the door and play Call of Duty with the sound off. Sometimes he'd read a book, maybe even do some of his homework, but that was rare.

"I'm really sorry," RJ's mom said to the police officers.

One of the officers took out a card and handed it to RJ's mom.

"Call this number on Monday morning to set up his court date. You'll also need to call the bowling alley to find out what the damage costs are going to be."

"Okay," RJ's mom said tiredly, trying to figure out how she was going to manage yet another burden her son had put upon her. He knew she wanted to have more energy, to really show that she cared about her son and that she was a good mom. She was just too tired and sick. Slowly, RJ was starting to feel something he hadn't felt yet… remorse.

"You'll also have to talk to the people at the cashier's desk to find out what his hospital costs are."

RJ's mom just shook her head as the officers told her to "have a good weekend." They walked out of the hospital. RJ was a free man.

RJ walked out of the hospital trying not to make eye contact with any of the people walking around or sitting in the hallways. For some reason, he had this thought that the whole hospital – the whole town – knew what he had done. He wasn't embarrassed … he had just started to get scared all of a sudden. Once he got home, he figured he'd be okay.

He followed his mom to the car and when they got inside, she started to cry. RJ just sat there. He didn't know what to do, but he hated seeing his mother like this. She was crying a lot more it seemed. He didn't really remember his father dying, but he was pretty sure he saw her crying when she found out he was dead. She hadn't dated much after that. RJ was always afraid she would get a mean boyfriend who would abuse her and beat him. RJ couldn't imagine leaving his mom and he didn't want to think about her leaving him.

This was why, sitting next to her in the car, he was starting to feel really bad. He looked at the cast on his arm and realized that, up until that moment, he hadn't thought about how expensive it would be. Then he started thinking about the other things his mom would be paying for. He tried to distract himself by focusing on the whiteness of his cast. He hoped this would drown out his mother's sobbing somehow. He started to imagine what might be written on it... how popular he would be in school if he let the other kids, the cool kids, sign it.

"I'm sorry, Mom," RJ finally said when it seemed like her crying had stopped for a moment. He had to say something else. This was all his fault. "I didn't mean to run through the glass door. Tim Craig and his brother were chasing me..."

RJ's Mom didn't say anything back. She just continued crying softly. She tried to wipe her cheeks, but her tears came down quicker than she could wipe them away.

They sat in the car for a long time. RJ looked out the window and saw people coming and going. It seemed like he had watched 200 people come in and out of the hospital in the time that they sat there.

"Something's gotta change." RJ's mom finally said. She was no longer crying. She turned on the car. "Something's gotta change."

Chapter 3.

RJ's mom was still asleep when he went out the next morning. He'd gone to his room right after he'd come home and played his old XBOX (he wanted a PS3 but his mom told him they couldn't "afford it"). Normally, playing video games made him feel better, but he had to adjust to playing with a cast on his arm. It was like a constant remainder of all the trouble he'd caused the day before. He thought he'd heard his mom on the phone, crying to whoever she was talking to, but when she'd called him to come and eat his TV dinner, she was no longer talking to anyone. Despite everything that had had happened that day, she'd still made him a Salisbury steak TV dinner and not one of the others in the freezer that he didn't like as much. His mom never ate with him.

He took off his Band-Aids, made sure the cuts weren't bleeding, and went outside. It was 11am and nobody on RJ's street was around. He'd played with a bunch of the kids that lived near him when he was younger, but a lot of parents had gotten this idea in their heads that he was a troublemaker. Nobody said anything at first; the other kids just started excluding him. Then finally, Steve Beaney, who'd moved to a nicer part of town two summers ago, told him that his parents didn't want him playing with RJ. He said it wasn't so much what RJ had done but what Joel had done. They figured that being his younger brother, RJ must have some of that in him. After that, all of the other families followed suit.

RJ didn't care. Yogi was his best friend, and when he wasn't around RJ could play video games and watch TV. That stuff was never going to go away. Yogi was usually around, though. Even though his parents didn't like RJ, Yogi didn't have many friends, and they weren't about to stand in the way of one he did have. They were very strict about knowing everywhere he and RJ went when they left the house. In fact, they always tried to set it up so that RJ and Yogi stayed in the house, preferably confined to Yogi's bedroom.

RJ lived in Bentonville, California. Like most cities, it had its good and bad parts. RJ's neighborhood wasn't that bad. At one time, it had been really nice when the small tract homes were built in the 1970s. The homes still looked nice, but the neighborhood overall was starting to look really run down: especially RJ's house. The small front lawn had large patches on it that were brown and dead. The outside paint job had faded considerably, and the inside was usually a mess. RJ and his mom wanted to keep their home clean, but since they rarely had people over, it was something that they let go. The house had a parlor area, a living room that was connected to the kitchen, and two bedrooms. The parlor and the living room each had a mess of papers, mail (mostly junk that they never got around to throwing away), clothes, and toys that RJ had either outgrown or broken. Yogi lived in a nice part of Bentonville, and Tim Craig lived in an even nicer part.

RJ's bedroom had some skateboard and video game posters on the wall. He also had a bunch of CDs and a CD player that only worked sometimes. He was mainly into heavy metal, but his main musical criterion was that it had to be fast. He wanted an iPod, but that was something else he knew he and his mother didn't have the money for. Like a lot of 13 year-olds, his clothes were all over the floor, along with his backpack, school books and everything else. Sitting atop all of this mess was his XBOX console. He hadn't bought it: Yogi had given it to him when he got a PS3.

As RJ turned the corner of a small strip plaza, he saw two kids that he knew: Danny Tran and Adam Mercado They weren't friends or anything, but they wouldn't give him any trouble. It seemed that it was only the big kids who messed with him, and if RJ couldn't hold his own with them (he'd won a lot more fights than he'd lost), he'd at least give as good as he got until he decided it was time to bail.

"What happened to your arm and your face?" Adam asked.

RJ held up his cast. The first feelings of pride about what had happened yesterday at Lincoln Lanes were starting to hit him. He was already in a lot of trouble, so why not try and enjoy some of the perks of his newfound fame?

"I broke it. At the bowling alley yesterday." RJ smiled.

"Oh yeah..." Danny said, his expression one of awe. "I heard about that... you ran through the front glass door! Are you in trouble right now?"

"Maybe," RJ started, like he hadn't given it a second thought. "I don't know. I have a court date but I don't know when. I gotta bail. Later."

RJ walked away.

"Bye RJ," Adam and Danny said.

RJ knew most of the kids his age were scared of him. That had pushed them away and made him something of an outcast. A cool outcast, but an outcast all the same. Joel had been an outcast, but he always had friends with him at all times.

It was a front. A brave front that RJ put up, and he knew it. It was something he did well so he didn't care if his only friend was Yogi.

As RJ passed the Family Four movie theater, he thought about going in and hanging out all day. It had four screens, and he and Yogi had spent countless summer days in there watching the same movies over and over. RJ walked up to the theater to see what was playing. He knew that the theater wouldn't have any new movies (this one never did), but for some reason he had an odd desire to be inside. Alone. In darkness. Then he stopped and started walking to Yogi's again. He'd left his money at home.

Yogi's house was 100% different than RJ's, which is why he liked hanging out there. Yogi's house had two stories, and it was always clean. The pantries were always stocked with food, and, if Yogi's parents weren't home, RJ would usually help himself to whatever drinks or leftovers were in the refrigerator.

Today Yogi's parents were home, so he and RJ hung out in his room drinking juice boxes (RJ's favorite flavor was grape, but all they had in the pantry was apple) and playing video games.

"Are you worried about seeing Tim at school on Monday?" Yogi asked. As good friends as RJ and Yogi were, Yogi could only worry about the things he knew about. RJ had never really talked to him about his mom being sick, how worried he was about his brother being in jail, or how scared he was about someday ending up alone. He couldn't talk to Yogi about these things. Yogi looked up to RJ, and if his strong façade was ever dented, Yogi might not need RJ anymore. In a lot of ways, when he really thought about it, RJ needed Yogi a lot more than he cared to admit.

"No," RJ said as he watched his video game soldier try to shoot Yogi's soldier. They were playing some knockoff, less violent version of Call of Duty. RJ didn't even know the name of it. He thought it was stupid that Yogi's parents said one video game was okay but another one, just like it, wasn't. Sometimes, RJ would make fun of Yogi for this, but that was rare. "It's not like he jumped me. I jumped him."

"What about his brothers?" The lisp in Yogi's voice made it trail off a bit.

"If they get me, they get me... but they'll have to catch me, first. And that's not gonna happen."

They played the video game for a little bit longer.

"I'm starving," RJ stated.

14.

"I can ask my mom to make us some sandwiches," Yogi offered.
"Nah." He didn't want to tell Yogi it was because he didn't like being around his parents. RJ and Yogi had only gotten in one argument in all the time that they'd known each other. Yogi got upset at a comment RJ had made about his mom's overbite. Yogi even stopped talking to him for a few days, and eventually RJ apologized.
"Lets go somewhere and eat. I want some pizza."
"Okay," Yogi said
"We've gotta go by my house. I don't have any money."
"That's okay," Yogi started. "I've been saving up my allowance to buy the next Zelda game. I'll use that."
"Cool," RJ said.
Yogi was always selfless towards RJ. That's why he was his best friend.

Chapter 4.

Somewhere between going to Yogi's house and going to the Hartsfield Pizza Shop, RJ's arm had started hurting in his cast. He didn't understand why, and it wasn't that painful, but it was there and RJ felt it.

The pizza shop was located inside the mall. It was a Saturday so it was fairly busy, and one thing RJ always noticed: no matter how bright it was outside, the pizza shop seemed like a dark cavern. That was one of the things RJ really liked about it. He could go there and not be seen. He could disappear inside the shop and feel like he had abandoned the world behind him until he decided to leave.

RJ and Yogi had both ordered two sodas and two slices of pepperoni pizza. It seemed like not a month had gone by since they'd become friends that they hadn't eaten there at least twice.

"Yogi, I'm not gonna go to jail." RJ's mouth was full of pizza.

"How do you know? What if at that court thing they put you away?" Yogi really sounded scared.

"If they wanted to arrest me they would have arrested me at the hospital. Stop worrying about it."

"Maybe we should start eating lunch on a different side of school?" Yogi took a large bite of his pizza.

RJ almost laughed after Yogi said that. The two of them didn't play with any other kids, really. In fact, both of them got letters sent home for being "antisocial." Yogi's parents had talked with him about making more friends. RJ just threw his letter in the trash.

At that moment, one of Tim Craig's best friends, Roger Rivera, sat at the table across from them with his dad. Roger seemed focused on carrying the pizza, so he wasn't paying

16.

attention to anything else. His dad held the drinks. So much for not being seen in the pizza shop, RJ thought.

"Look, I'm not gonna hide from Tim Craig, especially after I just beat him up." RJ glanced over at Roger to see if he'd noticed them yet. He hadn't. RJ wasn't scared of Roger, but he wasn't looking for trouble either.

"Well, I just hope it's over now."

"It is. For awhile, anyway."

RJ took a small bite of his pizza. Something about Roger being there had made him not so hungry anymore. He meant it when he told Yogi he wasn't scared, but seeing Roger so soon after what happened at the bowling alley had put him on even higher alert than normal. RJ had been jumped a few times, but even when that happened he'd managed to get in a few good shots before either getting beaten up or running away. He hadn't always been so tough, or so on his guard. It just seemed like once kids started messing with him they didn't stop. Since a lot of the kids who messed with him were all talk, RJ usually ended up getting in trouble because he hit them for "no reason."

"Hey, isn't that Tim's friend, Roger?" Yogi whispered.

"Yeah." RJ was amazed at how slow Yogi was to see potential problems.

"What if he sees us?"

Yogi may have paid for lunch, but he was starting to really get on RJ's nerves with all of his questions. Most of the time he wasn't this much of a wuss, but today it was like he was going out of his way to act like that. To his credit, Yogi was loyal and that was a big reason why RJ put up with him when he got nervous.

"Hey Roger," RJ said, smiling at Yogi. He wasn't trying to be a jerk; he just wanted to show Yogi that he was worrying too much.

17.

Roger's father motioned to him that somebody was calling his name. Roger seemed to go white when he saw that it was RJ.

"What's up?" RJ's smile faded as he stared at him.

"Nothing," Roger said.

"That's cool." RJ was slowly getting back the sense of cockiness that he had had at the bowling alley yesterday. "How's Tim?"

"I don't know. I haven't spoken to him." Roger pointed at RJ's cast. "What happened to your arm?"

RJ was taken by surprise. He'd have thought that everyone would've known about what happened at Lincoln Lanes by now. A kid in the 7th grade running through a glass door was big news. Those other kids knew about it...

"Roger," his dad busted in. He wasn't even looking at RJ. "Tell your friend that we're eating now."

I can see that, RJ wanted to say, but didn't.

"See yeah," Roger said, and turned around.

RJ looked at Yogi, who wore the same blank expression he always had. RJ turned back to his food. He was about to take another bite of his pizza, but decided he couldn't eat another bite.

Chapter 5.

The sun was coming down as he and Yogi walked home. RJ and Yogi had seen two movies. They had paid to see Diary of a Wimpy Kid 2 but then they snuck in to see Red Riding Hood. RJ had been a little distracted because of his meeting in the pizza parlor with Roger. It didn't last long.

There was something about the movies that made RJ forget about everything else. It was only in a dark theater that he was really able to concentrate. If they taught school in really dark classrooms he'd have all A's, he figured. RJ knew he wasn't dumb, but he was in mostly "special" classes because his mind was always in a million places. He was supposed to take some medicine to help him focus, but his mom never got it for him. As a result, he couldn't focus; his teachers thought he was stupid and they treated him that way. He didn't care. He didn't see the point in school anyway. He didn't know what his future held, but he wanted to work with Joel in some way.

Aside from a dark movie theater, he could always concentrate right before and during a fight. Yogi once told him that when RJ fought, he looked like a different person. He seemed bigger and taller and his eyes got really wide.

As they walked home, RJ started to think about Roger again. If nobody knew what happened between him and Tim Craig, did that mean that nobody cared? Then RJ realized that once more kids saw his cast that would speak for itself. He could tell them what happened. If he did it right, he could turn it into one of those legendary stories. It would be like the ones Joel used to tell. Like the time three guys outside a 7/11 had tried to jump him and Joel beat them all up. Or, how one time when Jason Sharkey, a guy three times Joel's size, tried to jump him in a bathroom. Joel ended up beating Jason to a bloody pulp as his friends stood helpless, locked out from getting inside to help him. Once more people found out what happened, RJ was sure that they would care about his cast.

"What are you gonna do tonight?" Yogi asked.

"Watch TV and play video games." RJ hadn't thought about what he was going to do later. He never did.

"You wanna spend the night?"

"Nah," RJ said. "My mom wants me to stay home because of what happened yesterday."

"Ohhh...."

That was a lie. RJ's mom hadn't said anything about wanting him to be home. She was sleeping when he'd left that morning, and chances were she'd be sitting in front of the TV when he got home. RJ wouldn't have minded staying over at Yogi's, but for some reason he wanted to be home tonight. He always had a thought in the back of his head that if he ever did anything really bad (and what happened at Lincoln Lanes would surely qualify), he might come home sometime and his mom would be gone. RJ didn't know when he first started to worry about this, but he found himself thinking about it a lot more lately.

Also, the last thing RJ needed was Yogi's parents questioning him about the cast, and then he would have to explain how he got it. They'd probably send him home. On top of that, RJ's arm continued to hurt. He wanted to get home and take something for it. He didn't know what, but he figured it would probably be the same stuff his mom took for her headaches. He sure hoped it didn't hurt like this for the four weeks the cast was supposed to be on.

"RJ!" A voice called to him. He and Yogi both looked in the direction of the voice, and RJ could immediately feel Yogi getting nervous. RJ instantly got in the stance he always took if he thought he might get in a fight. He was comforted by the thought of his cast. He figured he could bash anybody who came at them.

It seemed to have gotten dark really quick. Even with the lights of the street starting to come on, RJ couldn't make out where the voice was coming from until a big figure come out of nowhere and grabbed him.

"Hey!" RJ yelled as he was quickly picked up off the ground. Yogi watched in terror as the person wrapped their arms around RJ and swung him around. RJ started to get ready to hit whoever this person was with his cast, but then he stopped. It was Ben Ross. Joel's old best friend. They had always hung out until Ben got married and his wife got pregnant.

"What happened to your arm?" Ben asked as he lit up a rolled cigarette.

"I got in a fight." If anybody would think this was cool, Ben would.

"What'd they hit you with … a bat? That's the problem with you Boynton boys. You think you can fight the world. That was always Joel's problem."

"He didn't have a bat," Yogi said.

"Who are you?" Ben asked as he spat some loose tobacco from his cigarette on the ground.

"That's my best friend, Yogi," RJ started. "I beat up this kid at the bowling alley. His dad and his brothers started chasing me. I wasn't looking and I ran through the glass door in the front."

"Shut up! You liar!" Ben laughed.

"How do you think I got all these scars on me?"

RJ pushed out his face a little and held out his arms. Ben looked him over as he took a drag on his cigarette. For some reason, he could see the scars better under the glow of the streetlight now that RJ had pointed them out.

"Man." He blew the smoke out. "When you scrap, you really scrap."

"That'll teach people to stop talking about me behind my back."

Ben laughed after RJ said that.

"RJ, if you keep this stuff up you're gonna end up fighting everyone who even looks at you."

RJ thought about that. He liked to fight, but more than anything he liked to win. There was no way he could fight everybody. He didn't want to. If anything, he needed more friends, not less.

"Yeah," was all RJ could manage to say.

Ever since yesterday, RJ had started to feel a whole lot older. It was quickly dawning on him that he wasn't a kid anymore and life really did have consequences.

Chapter 6.

After talking to Ben, RJ and Yogi walked to Yogi's house, and then RJ was alone. He didn't like being alone, but not because it was dark now. He didn't even like being home alone during the day. It always calmed him when he turned the corner to his house and saw his mom's car in the driveway. Or, if he was home alone in his room playing video games, he was calmed by the sound of her car pulling into the driveway.

RJ's dad had left the house and never come home. This probably explained why he was afraid that his mom would leave him in the same way. Despite all the trouble he caused her, his mother had always stayed by his side. She never really yelled at him but maybe she should have. Maybe that's what RJ wanted so that he had a reason to stop doing the things he did.

As it was, RJ depended on his mom because she never gave up on him. This was why he hated seeing her sick and he hated to disappoint her; yet, for some reason, he couldn't stop doing it. She was the safety net between him and the rest of the world and when she was gone...

He never wanted to think about that.

RJ walked into his house only to see his mom sitting in the front living room area with some old guy. He had on clothes that looked like they had been worn a lot. The old man had a very bushy, white beard. He had short, straight black hair that was pressed against his head by hairspray. The man's face had a lot of wrinkles on it. These wrinkles told stories, and to RJ this man looked like he'd been alive forever.

"So this is the boy?" The old man asked, staring right back at RJ. His tone was measured and deliberate. "You don't look so tough."

RJ was caught off guard by this comment. Who the heck was this old guy in his house talking to him that way?

"RJ," his mom started. "This is your grandfather, Thomas. He took the bus here. He's gonna be staying with us for awhile."

RJ stared at them and slowly nodded his head.

"Okay."

"I was thinking he could stay in your room ... because there's a bed in there." His mom was trying her best to be delicate, but RJ couldn't help but get defensive.

"Where am I gonna sleep?" RJ was trying to control his temper, especially after everything he'd put his mother through the day before. But this was his room they were talking about. His sanctuary ... and it was being taken away.

"Out here..." His mother's voice trailed off. She was realizing no matter what she said, RJ was going to be upset.

"You don't realize how lucky you are!" his grandpa started, a smile on his face. "When I was your age, I would have given anything to sleep out in the TV room; on a big couch like this!"

As his grandfather patted the couch, RJ turned and headed toward his room. Like the day before when he was about to fight Tim Craig, everything was starting to go black.

"WELL THEN YOU SLEEP OUT THERE!!!" RJ screamed. And he headed into his room...

The first thing to smash against the wall had been RJ's XBOX. He was in such a blind rage he didn't realize how angry he was, or that he was only damaging things he really cared about. He had always had his room. It was the only place in his life that was his. He could play video games, watch movies, or just sit in bed and stare at the ceiling, and there was nothing anybody could say or do about it. Many a day, RJ had chosen to just stay in his room. If Yogi was busy, he could just stay in there, secluded, only leaving intermittently to get food or go to the bathroom.

What did any of that matter now? He wondered.

His grandpa was going to get his room and RJ was being relegated to the couch. He hated the couch even though he'd never really slept on it. He would still have a TV, but he wouldn't have any privacy. He'd have no place to go to get away from the world. His whole life, all thirteen years, he had never had much but he'd always had a room to sleep in (he used to share it with Joel), and now he didn't even have that. To make matters worse, RJ couldn't even throw a proper tantrum because the cast on his hand was making it hard for him to grip anything. Still, he had managed to throw a lot of books, video games, and anything else he could get his hands on.

If his mom was going to give away his room, RJ wasn't going to give it to them without a fight. They were going to get it – adults always got what they wanted when stuff like this happened – but that didn't mean that RJ couldn't try and wreck as much stuff as possible. He could destroy the room just enough so maybe his grandfather would have to take the couch. Or, maybe … just maybe … he'd leave.

In his anger, RJ had thrown a heap of things around him in such a way that he had almost boxed himself in his room. Once he cooled down, RJ started to throw things around the room so he could at least get out when he wanted to. The problem was, he didn't want to leave his room, but he was hungry. He hadn't eaten since he and Yogi had had pizza, and that felt like hours ago. He'd even forgotten how bad he felt for his mom over what happened yesterday.

The bedroom door opened and RJ's grandfather was standing there. RJ looked at him and suddenly felt something he hadn't anticipated. Fear.

"Lordy," his grandfather said, looking around the room. "Me being here has really put a bee in your bonnet."

RJ just stared at him. He was holding a poster he had ripped up. Now he just felt silly.

"Your mother tells me you run through glass doors?"

One of the first people to know what happened at Lincoln Lanes and it's my Grandpa?!? RJ thought, starting to get even madder.

"So what?!?!" was all he could think to say.

"She also said you broke your arm punching some kid in the head."

"Yeah, I did."

RJ's grandfather continued to stare at him. He hated being stared at: especially by someone who he felt was trying to pick him apart ... find his weaknesses. If RJ could help it, his grandpa was never going to find them, and neither was anybody else.

"Well, the way I see it, you've got two choices. You can stay in here and continue to destroy your room. Or, you can pull yourself together, stop being a little crybaby, come out into the kitchen, and eat with your mother and me. We're having a pizza."

"I had pizza for lunch."

"So have it for dinner." His grandfather's tone went beyond stern. He didn't care if he was in RJ's house. He wasn't going to accommodate RJ any more than RJ was going to accommodate him. "Or not. But you gotta eat sometime." His grandpa walked back to the kitchen area.

RJ stood there for a moment and then slammed the door. He started to kick a bunch of his clothes and books around the room. At least he still had two good feet. RJ even started to scream a little bit, not really knowing what he was accomplishing. Despite hurting his feet and his legs by accidentally kicking his backpack full of books, this was making RJ feel good. And tired.

After a few moments, he dropped to the ground. It was only after he'd stopped moving around that he realized he was crying.

Chapter 7.

RJ would have probably slept better if he hadn't been so angry about the events of the night before. Nothing much really happened after he destroyed his room. He had been so tired, he just went to sleep. He had hoped to go the whole night without eating the pizza his grandfather had bought, but after holding out for as long as he could, at about 11 o'clock he woke up, snuck into the kitchen, and ate a couple of slices. He had to be really quiet because his grandfather was snoring on the couch in the living room.

As RJ ate the cheese pizza (Figures he wouldn't get pepperoni ... he probably knows I like it, RJ thought), he watched his grandfather sleep. His mouth was hanging open, and a low, dull snore emanated out of it. RJ couldn't believe how much he hated him. He didn't mind that he was here so much as how he just presented himself in the house. This was RJ's home, and there was no way he was going to just let this guy come into it and take over. No way. He'd burn it down before he let that happen.

For a second, RJ thought about walking over to him and pressing a pillow against his face so he couldn't breathe. Then, just as quickly as RJ had that thought, it was gone. RJ was many things, but he knew he wasn't capable of that. Ever.

He finished his pizza, walked back to his room, and realized he'd made such a mess that there was no way he could sleep on his bed. He started to get angry again, but he realized it had been his own fault. Nobody had forced him to go into his room and destroy it. RJ pushed as much stuff off of his bed as he could and lay down.

Resigned to his fate, RJ realized that if his mom wanted her father to have it, he could have it. They just better not expect me to clean it, he thought to himself. Eventually, he went back to sleep.

RJ stared at the ceiling for a little bit as he listened to the bodies moving around in the kitchen the next morning. RJ had left the door open so he could hear them really well. It was early, but RJ didn't know what time it was.
"He ate some pizza," his mom said.
"I told you I heard him go into the kitchen. I knew he would. Kids love pizza," his grandfather stated.
"I looked in on him this morning... I think he destroyed your room."
RJ had to hold back a laugh. "Destroy" wasn't the word. He had annihilated it. He started to feel bad about doing it, but then he remembered why he did it and he didn't feel so bad anymore. That was another thing his brother had taught him:

"Never forgive and never forget who your enemies are."

RJ listened as he heard a body walking in the direction of his room. RJ closed his eyes so whoever it was would think he was asleep. Soon, his grandfather was in the doorway, pushing the door open a little bit more. He could feel his grandfather looking around the room.
"Well, you sure did a number on this place. It looks like a tornado hit it." He laughed.
"Don't worry, Dad, I'll clean it up," his mother called from the kitchen.
"No you won't," his grandfather started. "He will."

RJ had hoped to continue biding his time pretending he was sleeping, but after about 30 minutes he realized he would probably die of boredom if he didn't get up. So he did, and for some strange reason, started to clean his room. He didn't do it to make his grandpa happy or to try and make a better impression (that probably wouldn't have worked anyway): he did it for his mother. He had given her enough grief this weekend, and it still had almost a whole day left.

As RJ was starting to put his things back in place, his grandfather walked in the room.

"You're not just putting everything in the closet, are you?" his grandfather's voice had a hint of humor in it, but RJ didn't want to give him the satisfaction of smiling.

"No," RJ said, pointing to a trash bag that was almost full. "I put most of the stuff in there that I broke."

"It's a shame to hurt yourself when you're trying to hurt someone else."

"Who cares?" RJ stated.

"Your mom for one. That's why she had me come here. Try and get you into shape."

"Well, I wouldn't hold my breath. Besides ... I'm already in shape."

"No, you're not." His grandfather's tone was very frank, and it bothered RJ that someone that didn't know him could think they did. "You're not even close. Back when I was your age, if I acted like you did last night, my mom woulda laid a licken on me and then my dad woulda finished the job."

"My mom doesn't hit me," RJ said. He didn't want to think about what his dad would have done if he would have been there last night. However, he doubted he would've cared enough to hit him. All RJ really remembered about him was his drinking, the alcohol on his breath when he picked him up, and how he was always on the phone with people either talking really fast or yelling about something. The only person close to a grown-up that RJ ever really listened to was Joel.

"Well, maybe that's the problem. Nobody's ever broken it down for you that way. Made you toe the line. You behave like a lunatic and nobody's reigning you in. I'd do it right now, 'cept your mom told me not to."

"You can't hit me! You're not my father!" RJ yelled.

"You got that part wrong, RJ. I can hit you; I am just choosing not to. But you act up like that again – even close to that – you'll see what happens."

His grandfather coughed a bit as he walked out of RJ's room. It was a hacking, old person's cough. RJ put more of his things away. He momentarily felt better when he reconnected his XBOX and saw that it was still working. As he continued to pick up his room, he thought about what his grandfather had said.

For a few moments, RJ contemplated destroying his room again.

Chapter 8.

"He said he was gonna beat you?" Yogi asked.

As usual, Yogi was making more out of RJ's story than he should've. However, RJ had done his fair share of embellishing. He'd made his grandfather sound more like a monster than anything resembling a human being. Also, RJ hadn't really gone into detail about what he'd done to his room.

"Yeah, but he's old, Yogi. If he ever tried to grab me, all I'd have to do is move away and he'd never get me."

RJ tried to focus on the game of Pokemon that they were playing. Normally, RJ would make fun of Yogi for still playing such a wimpy kid's game, but RJ loved beating him at it because it was actually a game that Yogi was somewhat good at. It got boring playing him at other games and beating him so easily. RJ could easily beat Yogi at any game as long as they weren't actually talking. The problem today was that RJ wanted to vent about how his mom had ruined his life by having his grandfather move in with them.

"So what are you gonna do?" Yogi asked.

"I might run away," RJ stated. He was mainly testing the waters, knowing that at the very least he would have Yogi worrying about him. Aside from his Mom, RJ didn't seem to have too many people in his life who cared about him, so when the opportunity came up to get some attention, he took it. Plus, he knew the last thing that Yogi would want would be to face the Tim Craigs of Banks Middle School without RJ there to back him up.

"Really???" Yogi got wide-eyed, just as RJ had expected.

"Yeah. I can always go live with Joel."

"Or your dad." Yogi said cautiously.

"Yeah," RJ said absentmindedly. He hadn't ever told Yogi or anybody else the truth about his father. It was almost like, if he said that he was dead out loud, that would make it more real than it needed to be.

It was only at Yogi's house that RJ seemed to miss having two parents. Even though overbearing, overly protective parents like Yogi's would drive RJ crazy, he realized he probably felt that way because he'd never had parents like that. Even so, he would never have two parents again (not real parents anyway), and he certainly didn't need his mom's deadbeat father trying to be his dad. RJ didn't know too much about him other than he was a recovering alcoholic who didn't have any particular place to call home. Why RJ's mom had called on him after so many years of him being out of the picture was a testament to just how bad things had become with RJ. The reality was that he was there now, and there was nothing RJ could do about it. He just hoped that he and his grandfather could stay out of each other's way.

Then RJ started thinking about his mom again. Maybe she was sicker than he knew? Maybe his grandfather had been brought in as some sort of last dying wish? Maybe she...

All this thinking, and Yogi's constant questions, had worn RJ out today. Normally, if his parents weren't home, he'd stay there all day and play video games, but RJ found himself leaving Yogi's before two o'clock.

Chapter 9.

RJ probably wouldn't have minded being in what was called a "Special Day Class" if the room was at least near all the other classes. It wasn't. The room was located way in the back of the school. It was attached to the equipment room where all the balls, jump ropes, and everything else were stored for PE. Making this room even worse was that it didn't even have a window. How were RJ and the other kids in the class supposed to be inspired by the sign on the wall saying "You Can Accomplish Anything" when they were basically being taught in a room that seemed like an afterthought? Although none of the adults ever said this, RJ felt like he was in with a group of kids who were being hidden so that they wouldn't make the school look bad.

It didn't help that RJ wasn't really close with any of them. There were about fourteen kids in the Special Day Class. RJ didn't have any problems with any of them. If push came to shove, he was probably the toughest kid in the room, but he wasn't the class leader or anything like Joel had been. The way Joel made it sound, the teachers were actually afraid of him. RJ wasn't treated that way. All his life, the teachers seemed to be hands off: as if the whole class was in a race and it was up to RJ whether he was going to keep up or not. He did his best in the "regular" classes. As much as RJ wanted to believe that it was because that was where he belonged, he knew it was because PE, Art and Computer Lab were easy.

The two people RJ talked to the most were Tommy Rodriguez and Rick Rodney, but he didn't really know them. They just always seemed to get assigned to class projects together by the teacher, Mrs. Gonzalez. She was the person RJ talked to the most. She had all the kids in the class on a behavior contract. They had to turn in their homework by a certain time and they couldn't be late. Mrs. Gonzalez didn't tolerate fighting, name calling (unless she was saying them), or bad words. As strict as she was, Mrs. Gonzalez always let RJ slide on his homework. She seemed to understand that RJ had trouble concentrating.

    Mrs. Gonzalez wouldn't let RJ slide on fighting however, and that was probably why she seemed so disappointed when she saw RJ with his arm in a cast. Mrs. Gonzalez was smart and involved with her students, and no matter what RJ said, he wasn't going to have a good excuse to explain this.

    "Good morning, RJ," Mrs. Gonzalez said after he walked into the room. To him it seemed like she was purposely not saying something about his cast ... his badge of honor.

    "Good morning," he replied.

    RJ took his seat in the front of the class. Everyone seemed to be going about their day like business as usual. He had been in class for almost five minutes, and aside from some looks, nobody had said anything to him about his arm. It had been like that outside when RJ was walking to class, but he was late and he didn't want to add a trip to the office for being tardy onto his growing list of problems.

    RJ wondered if Mrs. Gonzalez had told the class not to say anything because she didn't want to give him the satisfaction? Or worse, maybe the principal had told all the teachers to tell their students not to acknowledge it? RJ figured that Tim Craig's parents probably gave a lot of the money to the school, and the principal was scared that they wouldn't get any more if everybody thought RJ was cool because he beat up Tim. If this was the case, it would just be RJ Boynton's luck. He goes and breaks his arm, runs through a glass door and, aside from Yogi, he couldn't talk about it with anybody.

At lunch, RJ was both relieved and happy to find out that word of what had happened at the bowling alley had in fact made its way to most of the students at Banks Middle School. Lunch was the time RJ and Yogi would normally be left to themselves, today they were constantly talking to people. Whether it was some of the tough kids who wanted to check out his cast, as well as know what it was like to run through a glass door, or even if it was some of the pretty girls (the ones who normally ignored RJ because of his reputation), he happily obliged everybody as he enjoyed his time being a minor celebrity.

"That Craig is rich," Tommy Rodriguez said as he examined RJ's arm. He was known around school for being a really good fighter. He had been taking Jiu-Jitsu classes since he was eight. "His parents are gonna fully press charges."

"Who cares?" RJ said, hoping that he sounded like he meant it.

Yogi was sitting against a wall eating his lunch. He had heard RJ tell the story of what happened with Tim Craig so many times, Yogi could probably tell it himself. He didn't say anything to RJ though; he was having too much fun being popular.

"You better hope he doesn't get his brothers on you," Tommy went on. "Tim isn't tough, but they are."

Tommy could talk to RJ like this because they were two tough guys. There was a respect between them. RJ didn't really think of him as a friend, but they had an understanding. Seeing as how Yogi seemed to fawn over him, Tommy was a nice breath of fresh air. RJ just didn't want to hang out with him too much. In some strange way, he felt like if he did he wouldn't be special anymore. Just another tough guy hanging out with Tommy and his tough guy friends. Not like Joel, where RJ was brothers with the leader of whoever he was with.

"I'll get my brother on them," RJ stated.

Tommy looked at him, surprised. RJ knew that Joel had an almost mythological status about himself. He was a legend. Going to juvenile hall and then jail will do that for you.

"I thought he was in jail?"

"He got out a few months ago." RJ looked at his cast.

"He did?" Yogi asked.

RJ shot him a look to "shut up." Joel had gotten out and there was talk, for awhile, that he was gonna come home. It never happened. RJ didn't know where his brother was now. He had told Yogi that when his brother got out, he was going to come get him and take him on a cross country trip. Joel had mentioned doing something like that. When this didn't happen, Yogi never asked about it, and RJ certainly never brought it up.

"Yeah, he went out to Florida. He's got business out there," he lied.

"That's cool. My brothers talk about Joel all the time. They say he was bad ass."

"He is," RJ said proudly. "So am I."

Tommy smiled a little bit.

"You wanna sign it?" RJ held up his cast a bit. He reached into his pocket for a marker he had borrowed from Mrs. Gonzalez. So far about 15 people had signed it, but they hadn't written anything; they just signed their names. Then RJ realized that he hadn't had Yogi sign it yet. "You sign it after him, Yogi."

"Okay." Yogi's eyes lit up.

RJ gave the pen to Tommy. He stared at RJ's cast and started to laugh.

"What?" RJ asked.

"I don't know what to write." Tommy smiled.

"Just write…" RJ tried to think of something funny to say. He was racking his brain trying to think of anything that would be better than just a signature. He continued trying to think of something for Tommy to write and then found himself getting angry. "I don't know; just write something."

"Okay."

Tommy wrote something, and RJ could tell by how long it took that he was actually writing more than a signature. He gave RJ his pen back.

"See you later." Tommy walked away.

"What'd he write?" Yogi walked over to RJ so he could see it.

RJ tried to look at it, but due to where he wrote it he couldn't read it that well.

"I can't read it. You do it."

Yogi held RJ's arm and read what Tommy had written.

"To RJ, a real tough guy. Tommy."

For the rest of lunch, only a few more people came up to RJ after Tommy Rodriguez. It seemed that everyone who needed to know the story knew it now. RJ could already feel his fame starting to disappear. Pretty soon, he would just be RJ Boynton again. There would be no cool story about him. He would just be another kid in trouble.

Later that day, as RJ was leaving class, Mrs. Gonzalez called him to her desk. He slowly walked over to her as all the kids filed out of the room.

"So what is it? Are you stupid or something? How'd you not know the glass door wasn't open?" Mrs. Gonzalez couldn't help smiling after she said that. RJ knew she wasn't laughing at him; she was just trying to talk to him about what happened without giving him any credit for it.

"I didn't even see it," RJ started. "I wouldn't have run through a glass door on purpose."

"Oh RJ," Mrs. Gonzales said. "What am I gonna do with you?"

He didn't know what to say. RJ had heard that statement a lot throughout his life, and he never knew how to respond.

"Well, I hope you learned something."

RJ just shrugged. He wasn't trying to be defiant; just honest. What had he learned? Other than it probably would've been smarter to look where he was going.

"After I heard, I thought you'd be more banged up..." Mrs. Gonzalez looked him over. "Other than your arm and a few scabs, you look fine."

"Yeah..." he said, recalling his conversation with Ben Ross. "I thought I'd have more scars."

"You have scars, RJ." Mrs. Gonzalez started gathering her things off the desk. "They're just where nobody can see them."

RJ thought about that. He figured Mrs. Gonzalez was referring to his father and his sick mother. Maybe even Joel. RJ never thought about how the events in his life had affected him, but he wouldn't say he felt scarred. Then again... maybe he didn't know any better?

"Better choices," Mrs. Gonzales went on. "You need to make better choices for yourself, RJ; otherwise you're gonna spend your life having people make your choices for you."

Chapter 10.

A week later, RJ's grandpa took him to the dentist after school. RJ hated taking the bus when it wasn't for fun, but it was their only way to get there. His grandpa didn't have a car. He didn't seem to mind taking the bus, which bothered RJ even more. He had been really irritable since he found out that Tim Craig's parents were really planning on pressing charges. For some reason, he thought they might back off from this and then the whole thing would just go away. Nope. They were rich and they had to protect the things they had, like their son. What did they care if that made things harder on people like RJ and his mom, who didn't have anything?

What RJ was really worried about was how badly his mom had broken down in front of his grandpa as she wondered how she was going to pay for all the damage he had caused. What had gotten to him the most was that his mother, through her tears, had wondered why her two sons always put her in situations like this. He hadn't heard what his grandpa had said about it, but RJ doubted that it was good.

He stared out the window of the bus hoping that the ride would be over soon. RJ felt really uncomfortable sitting next to his grandfather and not saying anything. The problem for RJ was he didn't think his grandpa liked him. It was like he was only in the house to babysit RJ. That was how he paid her back for letting him stay there. Having his grandfather around was cheaper than a babysitter or sending RJ somewhere after school. The last time they had tried that RJ had been okay; then one of the kids wouldn't let him play handball and RJ broke his nose. There had been bills for that too…

"You hear much from Joel?" RJ's grandfather finally asked.

"Yeah: all the time."

"No, you don't." His grandfather stared at RJ. He half thought his grandfather was playing a game with him. Trying to make RJ laugh like he did the few times he saw him when he was younger. Then RJ realized that his grandfather wouldn't joke around with him now. In fact, the whole time he'd been here so far, RJ hadn't laughed once. "Your father would be ashamed at what a deadbeat he turned out to be. Not like he was any better."

RJ couldn't believe what his grandfather just said. Nobody ever talked like that about Joel; much less his father. Joel was a legend. The toughest, coolest kid in the neighborhood. He'd been in over a hundred fights and never lost. He knew how to make money and he made other people money. Everyone respected him. All RJ's grandpa was was an alcoholic. That's what his mom had told RJ years ago, and even though she said he didn't drink anymore, RJ had seen him sneaking a few sips from some bottles that were high up in the kitchen pantry.

"Well, if you know I haven't spoken with him, why did you ask?" RJ said.

"I wanted to hear you lie. See how good you were… see if it ran in the family."

"Aren't you in my family?"

His grandfather laughed after RJ said that.

RJ turned and looked out the window again. He always looked out the window whenever he went anywhere. That's how he could map out a whole day for him and Yogi on the bus. They could spend a few dollars and go all over town. As RJ looked out the window he, for some reason, didn't remember any of the buildings he was now seeing. Maybe it was because his mom had taken him to the dentist before and she went a different way. Or, maybe it was because RJ felt more alone than he could ever remember.

Surprisingly, the dentist hadn't been that bad. RJ, with the way his luck had been going, half expected the dentist to tell him every tooth in his mouth needed to be ripped out. But despite his lack of brushing, he hadn't had so much as a cavity. He just needed a regular teeth cleaning. Aside from scraping his teeth and gums really hard, the dentist also complained to RJ about his poor dental habits. He figured they didn't do this at the rich person's dentist. He bet Tim Craig never got yelled at for having too much plaque.

As they walked back to the bus stop, RJ suddenly felt very hungry. This look may have transferred to his grandfather, because without saying anything, RJ found himself walking into the Oak Pine Diner. RJ had driven by this place many times, but he'd never eaten there. It wasn't a fancy restaurant, but it was a sit down, family-type place, and RJ and his mom rarely ate out.

"Two?" the hostess asked. She was a black woman in her forties. She looked nice, but strict.

"Yeah," his grandfather said. Then, of all things, he genuinely smiled at RJ. Not the mocking smile he'd been giving him. This was a genuine, show some teeth, smile. "I'd gotten so hungry I almost forgot you were behind me."

"I'm really hungry too," RJ said, surprised at how good it felt to talk with his grandfather and not be arguing about something.

"Really? Even after the way they were picking at your teeth?"

"Yeah; it only hurt a little."

They followed the hostess to one of the booths.

"They didn't numb you up, did they?" his grandpa asked as they sat down.

"No."

"Good. Your mom'd never forgive me if I took you out to eat after your dental appointment and you chewed off your tongue!"

Then RJ's grandfather did something even stranger. He started laughing.

It wasn't until RJ was almost done with his food that a thought occurred to him.

He didn't have any money.

RJ knew that only being thirteen, his grandfather couldn't really expect him to have any money on him, but this fear grew stronger because he actually thought that they might be becoming friends. Now the bill would come and there was a chance that his grandfather had no intention of paying for him at all. Even though he was still hungry, he suddenly didn't feel like eating the rest of his fried chicken and mashed potatoes. A cold feeling flooded his stomach, and for a second RJ actually felt like throwing up. What if his grandfather didn't pay for him? What if he just left him in the restaurant and they called the police? With his upcoming court date, this was the last thing RJ needed now. He started imagining his mom coming to the police station to pick him up....

"He has to pay for me…" RJ told himself.

He started to get mad. At himself. He should have asked before he ordered. He knew that nobody just gave you things. The one thing he knew, it was something Joel didn't even have to teach him: don't expect anything from anyone. Sure, he liked to tell kids what Joel or his dad was going to do for him, but he didn't really think they would (especially since he made most of it up). This didn't stop him from getting his hopes up, and telling these people those things made him feel good.

"Boy, you must've been hungry," his grandfather said. He took a large, white pill, put it in his mouth, drank some water and swallowed it. He noticed RJ watching him. "For my diabetes ... I should've taken it earlier, but I forgot."

RJ looked at his plate. It still had some food on it, but he had devoured his meal. His grandfather wasn't even halfway done.

"Yeah, I didn't eat lunch at school today," RJ finally said.

"You didn't? Why not?" His grandfather sounded angry at him again.

"I don't know. I forgot."

RJ had woken up late and forgot to make himself a lunch. He had money saved and he could've bought lunch, but he was saving up to get Joel something for when he saw him next. RJ didn't know when that would be, but he'd missed his brother's birthday at least 3 times. RJ thought Joel might appreciate a "Welcome Home" gift.

"You forgot?" RJ's grandfather stared at him curiously. He was waiting for him to say something insulting. "Well, you're young. I remember when I was your age, the last thing I thought about was eating."

"What'd you think about?" RJ was legitimately interested. He didn't know anything about anybody in his family other than his mom, dad and Joel.

"How old are you again?"

"Thirteen."

"Well, when I was thirteen, I was more interested in comic books, candy and girls."

"Girls?" RJ was very surprised. He thought that some girls were pretty, but he never really thought about them that much. He seemed too concerned with taking care of himself to have time to do that.

"Oh yeah, girls! When I was your age, I'd have two or three going at a time. We didn't do much more than hold hands, but that was good enough for me."

"Yeah."

"Don't be in such a hurry to grow up, RJ. That'll get you in trouble. Like that boy that you got in this mess with; busted your hand. Your mom says you always act like you have something to prove. That kind of thing will get you in a lot of trouble. It already has."

"But he made fun of my mom…" RJ felt himself starting to get mad. His mom was his grandfather's daughter; even an old man like him could understand that.

"So?"

"I didn't even do anything to him." RJ hoped he didn't sound as angry as he felt.

"RJ, if you go around fighting everyone who bothers you, you're gonna end up with nobody in your life except you."

Nobody around RJ.

That thought had been in RJ's head. He never felt like he really had anybody anyway. And this was before he started fighting people. After his dad, his brother (eventually his mom) … who else was there for him to lose?

The waitress came over and put the check down on the table. RJ had forgotten all about that. Before his stomach could get tight again, his grandfather's veiny, sun-spotted hand picked it up. As he held up the check to see how much it was, RJ saw that each hand had a couple of small, dark red scabs on them. He started to take out his wallet.

"No," he continued as he started to sort through his money. "You don't need to prove yourself to anyone. No matter what any kid says."

He took out a few bills and put them on top of the check tray.

"I just don't like people talking about my mom," RJ offered.

"You think I like it? She's my daughter. But who really cares what someone says about you? Or your mom? People have been fighting over the crap that people say about each other's moms for years. Is it worth it for all the trouble you're in?"

RJ knew that it wasn't, but it was probably because he'd gotten in trouble. If he hadn't – if he'd have sacked Tim Craig and gotten away with it – he might feel differently.

"But she's sick," RJ stated. For a second, the way his grandpa looked at him, RJ wondered if this was the first time he had ever heard anything about it.

"Yeah," his grandpa said, putting his wallet away. "She is that. But ... I guess I learned something today."

RJ stared at his grandfather. He had never really had a good talk with an older person. Especially someone as old as him.

"You're not such a bad kid ... you've just had some bad breaks."

RJ got a little excited after his grandfather said that. While he didn't say it directly, it sounded like he might be saying that there was a lot more to RJ than anybody (even RJ) might know.

As they sat on the bus coming home, they continued talking. RJ got to tell his grandpa about how Tim Craig always teased him. His grandfather shared with him stories about trouble he'd gotten into when he was younger. He also told RJ what his mom had been like as a kid. This was really weird for him, because he couldn't imagine her listening to music and being wild with her friends. She was just a mom to him. It was such a good talk, in fact, that RJ didn't even really notice that his arm had started hurting inside the cast again. As the talk continued, RJ had a new feeling that his mom wasn't the only person who cared about him.

Chapter 11.

Even with the court date looming, things for RJ had surprisingly quieted down. His mom seemed much more relaxed having his grandfather there, and RJ continued to see that he wasn't so bad. They weren't best friends or anything, but RJ no longer minded having him around, and he wasn't even that bothered when he asked him if he had completed his homework or picked up his room. A lot of times, RJ would say that he had when he hadn't, but he was doing it more. Even when he said that he had done his homework, if he hadn't, he'd at least done a little of it, which was much better than doing none. RJ had even noticed a change in his "regular" teachers' attitudes toward him. It was nothing major, but they no longer seemed to look at him with as much contempt. In fact, RJ didn't feel like he was the only kid getting in trouble in school. When Mark Backus cursed out Quinn Nguyen, RJ had the unique pleasure of watching somebody other than himself get sent to the principal's office.

RJ hadn't totally turned over a new leaf. He got Keith Mendoza in a headlock after he accidentally hit him in the head with his backpack. The thing was, Keith was more scared of the teachers then he was of RJ, so he didn't tell on him.

RJ watched the cars going in the opposite direction as he and Yogi walked down the street. RJ's backpack was a bit heavier because it had a couple more books than normal. He would usually just let it dangle, only taking home one or two books from the teachers he knew were gonna check up on whether he'd done his work or not. A lot of times, there was nothing in the backpack at all.

"I think my grandpa is taking me to the movies today," RJ stated, proud of the fact that Yogi wasn't the only one anymore who had family members that took him places.

"Really? What are going to see?" With no fear over something RJ wanted to do, Yogi's lisp was barely audible.

"I don't know." RJ hadn't been to the movies since the Saturday his grandfather came to live with him. It had only been a few weeks, but it felt like a lot longer. On top of that, RJ's mom had forgotten to give him his allowance as well. Normally, he would've asked for it, but things had been going so good between him and his grandfather (besides, he paid for the things they did), the last thing RJ wanted to do was get everybody mad at him again. He knew that his mom would eventually remember and then he could hit her up for the weeks that she missed.

"I'd like to go to the movies today," Yogi said. He didn't seem to be inviting himself so much as stating what he was thinking.

"So come with us," RJ offered.

Even if his grandpa wasn't going to pay for Yogi, RJ knew for a fact that he had over fifty dollars in "Joel money" sitting in his piggy bank, so he could pay for it himself.

"I can't. My sister has a ballet recital."

"That sucks."

"Yeah, but we're supposed to go out to dinner after, and according to my dad, the place serves really big chocolate sundaes."

Chocolate sundaes?!?! Man, Yogi's life must really be dull if he's willing to sit through a ballet recital for that! RJ thought.

There were only three other people in the theater for the 3:45 showing of Battle: Los Angeles. Right away, RJ knew that going to the movies with his grandpa was going to be different than going with Yogi. It all began with where they sat. RJ liked to sit in the back and Yogi never complained. RJ didn't mind sitting around crowds of people. In fact, he preferred it because he spent so much time alone. He'd liked the back of the theater ever since Joel told him the story of these guys trying to jump him and a friend when they were on a double date.

"I wasn't thinking and they cheap-shotted me," Joel had told him. "Now, no matter where I am, I like sitting with my back against the wall so I can see everybody who comes in and out of the place."

When RJ and his grandfather first got in the theater, RJ instinctively went right for the back row, but his grandpa walked up three rows from the front. Figuring that he should sit with him since he had paid for the movies (as well as popcorn and a Coke), RJ reluctantly went over to where he was. Since the theater wasn't that crowded, RJ figured he should stay on his guard in case Tim Craig, his brothers, or someone else he might have problems with decided to get him.

The second thing RJ's grandpa did was eat during the movie; loudly. RJ almost never ate during the movies. Normally, no matter how hungry he was, he could sit in a dark theater and concentrate on what was happening on the screen without his hunger bothering him. It wasn't like this at all at home, but the few times he had eaten during a movie he came out of the theater very confused about the plot. It was as if he couldn't do two things at once. His grandpa seemed to swish the popcorn around in the paper tub, and for some reason whenever he took a sip of his soda, it made a loud sucking noise.

This wasn't even the worst thing he did during the movie! The worst thing was all the talking. It wasn't even to RJ... it was just out loud. At first, when he did it during the opening previews, RJ didn't pay too much attention. He figured he'd stop once the movie started. He was wrong.

"THAT WOULDN'T WORK!" his grandpa said over and over. Another thing he seemed fond of saying was, "THERE'S NO WAY THAT WOULD HAPPEN!"

RJ half wanted to give him an elbow, but he was his grandfather. If it had been Yogi he wouldn't have thought twice, but Yogi never did stuff like that. He was too concerned with what RJ thought of the movies. A lot of the time when they watched one together, RJ could feel Yogi looking at him, trying to see if he thought a joke was funny, a scene was cool, etc.

"THERE'S NO WAY THAT WOULD WORK!" his grandfather was saying for the umpteenth time. All RJ could do was slide down into his seat and hope that somehow, someway his grandpa got the message.

He didn't.

RJ did his best to pay attention to the movie. Sadly, about halfway through the film he was still waiting for the point where he could enter his own world. That place where he could simply watch the film and not think about anything else. No matter what happened in the movie, his grandfather wouldn't stop talking. RJ had resigned himself to not really knowing what was even happening.

"THERE'S NO WAY THAT WOULD HAPPEN!" his grandpa bellowed again.

"SHHHHHHH!!!" someone in the sparsely packed theater finally yelled.

RJ was nervous about how his grandfather might react, and for a second he realized that this is how Yogi must feel when the two of them went places. It was an awful feeling. He'd have to remember that. RJ's grandpa didn't even hear the guy. The talking continued...

"THIS MOVIE IS A PIECE OF CRAP!!!"
Suddenly, RJ's grandfather stood up and threw his soda at the screen. It splattered all across the middle of it.
"WHAT'S YOUR PROBLEM, OLD MAN?!?!?" someone else screamed.
"THIS MOVIE!!!" RJ's grandpa yelled as he moved past RJ and walked out of the theater under the red exit sign.
RJ watched all of this in shock. He had never expected anything like this in his life. Instinctively, he got up and followed after his grandpa. As embarrassed and angry as he had been with his constant talking a few moments earlier, RJ was now filled with a sense of pride about what he had done. In a strange way, it was as if he had somehow learned something about himself and his own temper. Maybe this explained why RJ got so mad sometimes? Why he never seemed like he could control his temper? RJ felt a sense of relief as he realized that there really were other people in the world like him.

RJ's grandpa walked by himself about 10 feet away. As far as he could tell he was still talking, but RJ couldn't make out what he was saying. As RJ watched him, he started to wonder what he looked like when other people saw him walking from behind.
Did he look like his grandpa? He wasn't nearly as old as he was, so he probably didn't slouch like him, but what did he look like to other people? Anybody who saw his grandpa now – in his ruffled clothes, with his bushy beard, talking to himself – would no doubt think he was crazy.
RJ wasn't dumb. He knew he didn't have many friends, and the friends he did have (other than Yogi) were really only acquaintances. He had never really thought about this, but lately he'd started wondering if he really had any friends. Including Yogi. After all, how close could they be when Yogi

seemed like he was scared of him all the time? In some ways, Yogi was more important to RJ than his mom because he was somebody who didn't have to be around RJ, but he was. If RJ didn't have Yogi, then he really wouldn't have anyone. Not even Joel because, even though he was Joel's brother, RJ couldn't really depend on him.

"You there?" his grandpa asked, jostling RJ out of his thought. He decided it was time to stop thinking about this stuff. If he thought too much, he might start getting scared... or angry. "My God! You're as white as a sheet."

It was only then that RJ realized he was sweating. The incident in the theater and everything he was thinking about had actually made him start to shake a little bit. He only remembered getting like this when he was about to fight someone ... then things would go black. He never remembered feeling that way when he was scared before.

"Yeah," RJ said softly.

"What are you scared of? I'm old. I can throw things at movie screens all day long. What are they going to do to me?"

RJ managed to smile at him. For some reason, he was having a hard time talking. He felt really nervous and he couldn't explain it at all.

"Are you mad at me?" RJ finally asked. He had no idea where that came from.

"Mad at you? No! I'm mad at that flaming movie! I can't believe they even call it that. It's a shame what passes for a picture nowadays."

"I didn't think it was so bad."

"That's because you're too young to have seen any good movies."

They started walking together. His grandfather seemed to calm down a bit.

"You ever seen Gone With The Wind?"

RJ shook his head. "I've heard of it," RJ offered. "In the book The Outsiders." He was sort of reading it for school.

"What about Stagecoach? John Wayne was in that one."

"No."

"Those were movies. They weren't just computers doing everything while the actors play pretend."

"What about Star Wars?" Everyone likes Star Wars, RJ thought.

"Star Wars?!?" RJ's grandpa half yelled. "That's the biggest computer movie of them all. I went to see it in 1977. Everybody said how great it was. I walked out half an hour in."

Normally, RJ would have argued, but he didn't want to argue with his grandfather even though his grandfather seemed like he wanted to. That seemed to be his way of talking. His way of getting close to people. The problem for RJ was he usually argued with kids who weren't as smart as him. Even if they were smarter than him, RJ knew that they'd never go all the way with it. That was because those kids feared him. This made RJ feel lonely again, so he decided not to think about it.

He watched his grandfather walk for a bit more. Finally, after about five minutes, his grandfather stopped and looked around.

"So where are we anyway?" he asked.

"We're about a mile from my house." RJ thought he should've said "our" house, but he didn't realize that until after he said it.

"What time is it?" His grandpa then answered his own question by looking at his watch. "Hmmmm ... it's a little after four. We could walk home, but we're out. I wonder where the action is?"

"Action?"

"Action!" his grandfather said with a smile. "Where it's happening or cool. Or, I guess another word I've heard some of you kids say is 'dope.'"

"I don't say that."

"You don't?"

"No."

"So what do you like to do, Russell?" So few people called RJ by his real first name, he was always surprised when he heard it. His grandfather stared at him, and RJ realized he hadn't ever really had a grown-up ask him what he wanted to do. Usually, they were talking at him or, in his mom's case, taking him to do something.

"I like playing video games."

"Video games?"

"Yeah: I play them all the time with my friend Yogi."

"Well, you've got a video game player at your house. No sense in me feeding those machines for something you can do for free."

His grandpa turned and started to walk again. RJ noticed some blood on his grandpa's arm.

"You're bleeding."

"What?" His grandfather looked at him. RJ pointed to his arm.

"Your arm is bleeding."

His grandfather looked at some blood coming out of a scab on his arm. He seemed to have a few scabs on each of his arms today. Like he'd fallen down in the street or something.

"Oh…" His grandfather took a handkerchief out of his pocket and started to wipe away the blood. "That's the problem with diabetes. If you bump your arm and it bleeds, it takes a lifetime to heal."

RJ's grandfather resumed walking as he held the handkerchief against his arm. Every so often, he'd look at the open scab to see if there was still any blood coming out of it. RJ walked side by side with him now.

Chapter 12.

RJ normally didn't pay attention to the mail that was on the table. Nothing ever came for him, and the things that did were usually just relating to him (health insurance, progress reports from school, etc.).

Today was different, however. The first letter that got his attention was the one from Lincoln Lanes Bowling Alley. He knew that it was about the sliding door he'd run through. He didn't know what was happening with that, but he knew his Mom wouldn't be able to pay for it. He had heard her talking to her father, and it seemed like she was on a payment plan of some sort. RJ wouldn't have looked at any of the other mail except, underneath that, he saw a letter that was addressed to him and him only. It was written in green ink. Then, in the left hand corner of the letter, there was an address that said "Rittner, California." Above that was the letter "J," a period, and the last name "Boynton." This was a letter from Joel.

Joel had written him. Finally.

RJ thought about telling his grandfather about the letter, but every time he had brought Joel up, his comments had been less than complimentary. His mom was lying down; otherwise, RJ would have surely told her. She would care about finding out where her oldest son was and what he was doing. Maybe things were going really good for him? They had to be… this was Joel Boynton, the coolest kid in Bentonville. If RJ had good news for her about him, this would make her happy.

He quickly went into his bedroom as if he was hiding something. RJ shut the door, sat on his bed, and opened the letter. For some reason, he found himself nervous even though he hadn't read a word yet. The letter read:

RJ,

    What's up, little man? It's Joel. I'm okay. Living in Rittner. I've been out for about 2 months. Tell Mom thanks for putting money on my books when I was in there. It helped out a lot. I'm gonna be visiting you soon. I might even stay for awhile if Mom is cool with it. I told all of the guys inside about you. They think you're a real cool kid. I'll probably call or something when it's time to head out your way.
    How are you?
    Your Brother,

Joel

    RJ was so excited, he reread the letter. If Joel moved back home and his grandfather was there, along with his mom, this would mean RJ would almost have a full house. He'd have a family. It may not have been exactly like Yogi's (or a lot of the kids' at RJ's school), but he didn't care. He'd have people around all the time and never be alone. Maybe Joel would get a job and contribute, and RJ could get a job and his mom wouldn't have to work so hard? She could rest more and maybe get the cancer out of her body?
    He decided to stop thinking about all of this good stuff. He was just happy to hear from his brother. At the very least, he'd come home, they'd go out on the town, and everybody would see RJ with his big brother. RJ wouldn't have to answer for why Joel wasn't around anymore. He'd be there and he could speak for himself. He could help RJ; talk to him about big brother things, like he used to do... sort of.
    RJ lay in his bed until his mom came home with some sandwiches from Subway. He had been so into Joel's letter that he didn't even hear her leave. She'd gotten him a sub with

onions (which RJ hated), but he decided to keep his mouth shut. No point in ruining what had been a great day. The only thing bothering him was, even after hearing from his long lost brother, RJ still didn't really know exactly where he was.

Chapter 13.

Cleaning the house on a Saturday wasn't RJ's idea of a fun day off, but his grandpa had asked him to, and he'd sweetened the deal by offering RJ $5 to do it. So far, he had saved $65 (most of it was money he already had) in his "Take Joel Out When He Comes To Visit" fund. Normally, he would have just cleaned the kitchen/living room and the parlor area, but his grandfather had told him to "take the vacuum all over the house."

He was just about done when his grandfather walked into RJ's mom's room holding two ice cold sodas.

"I was saving these for a special occasion," he said over the noise of the vacuum cleaner.

RJ had been vacuuming up the last section of his mom's room. He turned it off and took the soda from his grandfather. They both sat down on the bed. RJ had been so busy cleaning, he hadn't realized how hot he was. His grandpa hadn't been doing anything at all and RJ noticed beads of sweat on his brow and upper lip. He took a big drink of his soda and let out the refreshed noise that old people make.

"Now that's just good. I can think of few things better than a cold soda on a warm day."

RJ took a drink from his soda and was also surprised at how refreshing it was. For some reason, he looked at the can and took notice of the layer of cold water coming off of it.

"Isn't it true, if you were in the desert and somebody gave you an ice cold Coke to drink, like this, that would make you thirstier?" RJ couldn't remember where he'd heard that, but he remembered being surprised when he did.

"I imagine that it would, but I'll tell you what, if you're dumb enough to be in a desert without water, you'd better take any cold drink that comes your way!" his Grandpa laughed.

"I guess the best thing to drink is water. Even if you aren't in a desert."

"Water? It's okay, but it doesn't taste like anything. This doctor I used to see used to always tell me that I needed to drink more water. Said it was why I kept getting kidney stones. So I did. I drank gallons and gallons of the stuff: then I got another kidney stone!" He laughed again.

"What's a kidney stone?"

"It's bad. Let me tell you that. Hurts like nothing you've ever felt. After drinking all that stuff and getting another stone?!? I told that doctor what he could do with his water."

RJ laughed and his grandfather smiled at him.

"You're a young pup. You don't have to worry about things like that, but when you get to be my age you really feel it when you have something wrong with you."

"Yeah," RJ held up his arm. Over the past weeks, his cast had gone from being an almost shiny white to a dark, cream color. "This is the only thing that's ever really gone wrong with me."

"That didn't go wrong; you did it to yourself."

"I didn't mean to," RJ said sheepishly. Other than that time after the dentist, he and his grandfather hadn't talked about what had happened at the bowling alley. It wasn't lost on RJ that had that event never happened, his grandpa probably wouldn't even be living with him.

"Well, you did it just the same. Hopefully you've learned something from it. People are gonna talk about you. Let them talk. Words never hurt anybody."

RJ had been hearing that phrase his whole life, but he didn't believe it. Words had hurt him more than punches or kicks ever had. People making fun of him for being poor. People laughing at him because he was in "special" classes. Kids making jokes about him only having one parent at "Back to School" night (that was when his mom felt well enough to go). People saying things about him that they didn't think he could hear. There were also things that weren't said that hurt too. Like when he'd go to the store with his mom and she'd move really slow through the checkout line. People would be staring at them and he'd want to hit each and every one of them.

"It just makes me mad when people make fun of me," RJ finally said.

"Why?"

"Because it does... do you like it when people make fun of you?"

"Well, you're in grade school, so it makes sense, I guess. Kids can be mean, but don't think that just because you get older it changes all that much. Who knows? You'll probably have it out of your system by then." His grandpa took another big drink of his soda.

"What do you mean? My system?"

RJ could usually follow the things his grandpa said, but this sounded like something he probably should get some clarification on, just to make sure.

"Well, you've got a lot of anger in you. You've got a right to that, seeing the shakes you've had in your life, but it's the kind of thing that, if you don't deal with it, will get you in even more trouble."

"If I could go back to that day, I don't think that I would run through that door."

"You shouldn't have been running from the kid you beat up." His grandfather's voice was very stern.

"I couldn't let Tim Craig and his brothers get me!" This was something nobody seemed to understand but RJ.

"What I mean to say is, that you shouldn't have been fighting. You're too smart for that, RJ, and you know it."

RJ wanted to remind him about what Tim had said about his mom, but his grandpa had already made it clear that he didn't care about that. Besides, it wasn't every day that people called him smart, and he was just sort of enjoying the rarity of the moment.

"When is your court thing?" If this was his grandfather trying to change the subject to avoid a possible argument, he wasn't doing a very good job.

"I don't know. It's soon, though."

"Are you scared?"

"I don't want to go to juvenile hall. It wouldn't be so bad if Joel was still in jail and they sent me to where he was."

"They won't send you there," his grandfather laughed. "You're too young ... and besides, you have to be really stupid to go to that place."

"I've been trying not to think about it," RJ lied. He had been thinking about it. A lot. He was scared that he would be sent away, and when he came home his mom wouldn't be there anymore. He'd be on his own ... a criminal. How would he survive?

"Well, I would if I were you. I'd start thinking of ways to walk the straight and narrow. To show that judge that you're not a punk."

"I'm not a punk," RJ said, starting to feel the old anger at his grandpa come back. "I've been doing really good in school since everything happened."

"And I, and your mom, appreciate that. But you can't just say it and you can't just do it for a little while. You've gotta commit to being a good person. All the time. Then maybe the word gets around that Russell James Boynton isn't just someone going around looking for trouble. You continue to get good marks in school, be polite, turn the other cheek when you can ... trust me, things will work out for you."

"Maybe," RJ said, not sure how much he believed it, but not really wanting to think about it anymore. He would have his day in court soon, and just hoped that he wouldn't have to leave his mom and grandpa.

It was around 2:30 that Yogi came over. RJ hadn't remembered inviting him, but it always seemed like whenever they even mentioned hanging out, Yogi took it like they were definitely going to do something. Normally with his mom, if she was home, RJ would've simply told her he was going out with Yogi, and before she could respond, he would be out the door. Now, with his grandpa there, he couldn't do that. It wasn't just because his chores weren't done and he wanted to keep RJ accountable (they actually were done); it was because he and his grandfather had been spending a lot of time together, and RJ didn't want him to think he was ditching him.

"So you're Yogi?" his grandfather said as Yogi and RJ played video games. He was standing in the door of RJ's bedroom watching the two boys play Call of Duty. They were switching off between guys.

"Yeah," Yogi said. Between RJ's grandpa and having to focus on the game, he was really playing lousy today. This was why RJ had never had Yogi back him up in a fight: he couldn't focus on more than one thing at a time.

"How'd you two boys meet?"

RJ realized he probably should've warned Yogi that his grandpa was a little weird, but he was actually curious what Yogi's answer would be, because he had forgotten how they met.

"I don't remember," Yogi said. He sounded really nervous now. RJ wanted to tell him that he didn't have anything to be nervous about, but he didn't want to make Yogi any more uncomfortable than he was.

"You've just always been friends?" His grandfather folded his arms and smiled.

"Yeah, I guess."

"I'm not your friend now," RJ laughed. "I want you to die so I can play."

Yogi looked at the screen and saw that he had just been killed. RJ took the XBox controller from him.

"Oh man!" Yogi cried. "That's not fair. That game didn't count, RJ. I was talking to your grandpa."

"Yes, it did." RJ was surprised by Yogi's sudden defiance.

"It shouldn't. I wasn't even playing, really."

"Well, it does," RJ stated, pressing the button on the controller to continue the game.

"Video games ... you kids will spend your whole lives playing those things, and for what? You get a high score, but what have you done?"

"It's just for fun, Grandpa."

"Yeah," Yogi offered. "Plus, there are people that their job is to play video games. They make a lot of money."

"I'd love to have that job," RJ said, imagining what it would be like to get to play video games all day. He'd be in paradise.

"Job? That ain't a job!" RJ's grandpa raised his voice considerably. "Building things. Doing physical work, using your mind: that's work. All you kids are doing is pressing buttons."

"We're not; you really have to think as you play this game." RJ said.

"Oh, come on..."

"You do. Here ... play one of my guys."

RJ held out his controller to his grandfather.

"No...." he started to say.

"Play, Grandpa. I just want you to see what the game is like."

"Okay."

He took the controller from RJ and moved a little closer to the boys, but he didn't sit down. He examined all the buttons.

"What the hell is this?" he asked as he pressed some of them.

"Don't worry about that. This game is Call of Duty. It's a war game. You'll like it. It's like you're living it all over again."

RJ and Yogi laughed.

"I wasn't in any war! I don't believe in them." He continued to stare at the controller, trying to figure out what the tiny letters said. As he started to click around on it, RJ's grandfather suddenly heard explosions and gunshots coming from the game.

"You've got to start killing people, Grandpa!" RJ laughed.

"The buttons on the right fire, and you move your guy with the controller on the left," Yogi said. His lisp was really pronounced as he tried to speak cautiously.

RJ's grandfather started to randomly press buttons and actually killed some people.

"Grandpa!" RJ said excitedly. "You killed some guys."

"I did?" RJ's grandpa was truly bewildered by this whole experience.

He stopped pressing the buttons and just stared at the screen. At that moment, one of the enemies appeared in the distance. He lobbed a grenade, and when it exploded, his portion of the screen turned red.

"What the heck just happened?"

By this point, RJ and Yogi were laughing so hard, they had lain on the floor and couldn't speak. The game resumed play, but RJ's grandfather had had enough. It was bad enough not knowing what was going on, but he didn't need to be laughed at by kids who did.

"Stupid. These games are a stupid waste of time." He set the controller on the TV and walked out of the room.

As Yogi and RJ continued to laugh on the floor, RJ realized he couldn't remember the last time he had laughed so much.

RJ, his grandpa, and Yogi walked down the street together. It was a little after 3:30, and after deciding that there was nothing to eat in the house, RJ's grandfather offered to take the boys to get some pizza.

"I'm telling you, Grandpa," RJ pleaded. "If you practiced for like, 20 minutes each day, you could get good at Call of Duty, and then we could play together."

"You just need to play a lot. That's how we got good," Yogi said.

"No way. I'm not gonna waste my time. Pushing buttons, blowing things up, killing people that aren't even real. There's too much real life stuff going on for me to do that. You boys should read more books!" His grandpa's tone was definitive, but RJ still thought he might change his mind.

"I don't ever see you reading," RJ smiled.

"That's because I do it at night when you're counting sheep. I like to read when it's really quiet. I sit back with a book of short stories, and I let my imagination go wherever the story takes me. It's fun, it's free, and you don't have to push buttons."

"Well, it's not really free. You gotta buy the book."

RJ stared straight ahead, and the smile on his face started to fade.

"RJ, look..." he heard Yogi whisper. For a quick moment, he felt a sense of pride in the fact that Yogi was always trying to help him. Who cared that RJ had already spotted a potential problem long before him? Most of the time, RJ felt alone in the world, and he would take all the help he could get.

Tim Craig and his brother Mike were riding their bikes on the other side of the street. Mike was in the 11th grade, and he was known for being really tough. Joel had six years or so on him, and RJ sure wished he was here right now. He could probably beat up Mike and Larry at the same time.

RJ didn't want to call attention to himself, Yogi, or his grandpa, but at the same time he couldn't take his eyes off of them. This was all he needed. The first really good, normal time he could remember having, and now it might be ruined.

"What are you two so quiet for?" His grandfather's voice broke into RJ's thoughts.

There was a chance that Tim and Mike might walk right past them; that they wouldn't notice RJ, Yogi, or his grandfather. Then RJ started thinking again about what might happen if they did notice them? Would they start a fight? Would they beat up RJ's grandpa? He started getting himself ready if there was going to be a fight. That feeling he hadn't really felt since the bowling alley. He didn't miss it, and when it started up again, it made his whole body dip down a little. As if he was getting sick.

"That's the kid RJ beat up at the bowling alley," Yogi said.

"Yogi…" RJ didn't want to remind his grandpa what a bad kid he was.

"Which one?" his grandpa asked.

"The shorter one. That bigger one is his brother," RJ said, hoping Yogi wouldn't give his grandfather any more information. He never seemed to know when the right time to talk was.

"Hmmmm…" his grandpa said, looking at both boys. "I guess they made kids meaner looking back in my day."

"Well," RJ started. "I beat up that little one easy. It's his big brother that I'm worried about now."

As much as RJ didn't want his grandfather to think he was a bad kid, he didn't want him to think he was a wimp, either.

"They're the family that has that case on you?"

The case.

It always seemed like, just when RJ had managed to put that out of his mind, something happened to put it back there again. For some reason, he held out that there might be a turn of events that would make the whole thing go away. It had gotten so bad that he'd even thought about praying for that to happen. RJ didn't even know what religion he was; he just knew that, in some way, despite everything that had happened to him throughout his life, he knew about and he believed in God. Whether God was a man or woman, he didn't know, and he didn't care. As far as he was concerned, there might be many Gods like in all those Greek Mythology books he'd heard about in school. He just hoped that, when he prayed, the right one would hear him.

And then, as if God or some other form of good luck was on his side, Tim and Mike Craig rode past them. RJ's thoughts of some big fight between himself, Yogi, his grandpa, and the Craig Brothers were just that. He glanced over at his grandfather, who was still staring at Mike and Tim. RJ decided not to answer any questions about the case. Like his dad, if he spoke about it, that made it more real than it needed to be ... at least for now.

The pizza parlor at the mall was lively that late afternoon. RJ had made sure that they were in an area where there would not be too many other people around. They had gotten a pepperoni and sausage pizza. RJ would've been just fine with pepperoni, and Yogi would have been happy with cheese, but his grandpa wanted both, and since he was paying, that is what they got. RJ started thinking that maybe for his grandpa's birthday (whenever that was), if he could afford it, he'd buy him a gift and take his grandfather and his mom out to eat.

"So what do you boys do all day when you're not pretending to go to school?" his grandpa asked, taking a bite of his pizza and washing it down with some soda.

"We play video games, go to the mall, walk around..." RJ was trying to think of more things he and Yogi did together, but he couldn't. He and Yogi never seemed to think too much about any of the things they did; they just did them.

"Sometimes we take the bus places," Yogi offered. He took a sip of his soda and wiped his mouth.

"Yogi," RJ's grandpa started. "I used to have a friend just like you when I was RJ's age. We did everything together. He was the best friend I ever had."

"Yogi's my best friend," RJ stated.

Yogi looked at both of them. All of this praise was coming so quick, he didn't seem to know how to react.

"I know," his grandfather said. "I've heard people say that if you go through this life having one really good friend, you're lucky. You're a good friend, Yogi. RJ's lucky to have you."

Yogi, his mouth hanging open a bit now, looked at RJ. He still didn't know what to say.

After their meal, they walked around the mall. RJ realized that, except for the non-incident with the Craig Brothers, he couldn't remember the last time he felt this good.

Chapter 14.

RJ's arm seemed to look a lot smaller than it had before the cast was put on it. He had heard from some kids who had broken their arms that this might happen, but with the cast still on his arm he didn't really think about it. Surprisingly, the whole time that he had had the cast on, it hadn't ever really itched that badly. When it had first been put on, Yogi told RJ that it was going to itch (he had broken his arm a few years ago when he fell off his bed!). In fact, Yogi had wanted to come to the doctor to see what the inside of the cast looked like after being on his arm for two months. He hadn't been able to because his parents were going someplace and he had to go. So it was just RJ and his grandpa.

"Move your arm slowly," Dr. Phong instructed RJ.

RJ moved his arm back and forth. At first, he felt a sharp pain in his elbow, but the more he moved it, the more it seemed to go away. He looked at the cast that had been cut off his arm. The inside had a dark, yellowish, brown color.

"How does that feel?" the doctor asked.

"It hurts a little," RJ said.

"Just keep moving it."

RJ did, and he looked at his grandpa.

"Well, you've got two arms again," he stated.

"Yeah," RJ said.

"Let's keep it that way. No more running through buildings or whatever it was you did."

"I know," RJ said.

His mom usually never lectured him in front of other people. She wasn't around that much, but even when she was, she never said anything. She just sort of listened to what people said, but it was never clear if, while she was nodding her head, she actually heard it.

"You notice that your right arm is smaller than you left one now?" the doctor asked as he made some notes on a chart.

"Yeah," RJ said, holding them side by side so he could really see the difference. "It won't stay like that, right?"

"For a little bit." Dr. Phong started to examine RJ's right arm. It really looked small, almost as if during its time in the cast, it had all the blood and muscle sucked out of it.

"Maybe it all went into the cast, and that's why it smelled so bad," RJ wondered.

"I often tell people to wear a long sleeve shirt or a jacket if that's something that's going to make them self-conscious."

"Ohhhhh." RJ hadn't thought about that. He always felt different around most of the kids (even Yogi sometimes), but he didn't ever think he might look different ... until now.

RJ looked out the window of the bus as he leaned against his grandfather a little bit. Every so often, RJ looked over at him and noticed he was drifting in and out of consciousness. RJ looked at the scabs on his grandfather's arms and hands. Most of them were closed up, and the open ones had Band-Aids over them. He wondered if these scabs hurt his grandfather.

"Why don't you take a picture?" his grandpa said. RJ hadn't realized how hard he had been leaning against him, and that in order to get a better look he'd probably woken him up.

"Sorry." RJ moved back into his own seat a bit more.

"I suppose when I was your age I probably would've looked at open scabs and bloody arms too."

"Do they hurt?"

"Nah ... sometimes. If I put that ointment crap on them that's supposed to help me. Sometimes your mom tells me to put things on them, but I usually just bandage them up or put on long sleeves when I'm around her."

They sat there for a moment. RJ wanted to ask if a lot of blood got on his clothes when he wore long sleeves, but he didn't. He thought it probably did.

"You figure that's what you're going to do with your arm?" his grandfather asked as he motioned to it.

"I don't know," RJ said, only really thinking about it now. It did look weird, but he wasn't sure he had any long-sleeve shirts he liked; especially ones that didn't have buttons on them. On top of that, he hated to wear jackets, and the one jacket he did have was handed down from Joel. He had liked wearing it a few years ago (especially when Joel left town and some people saw the jacket and mistook RJ for him), but it was starting to fall apart.

"You think that Craig kid will give you any guff over it?"

"Probably not," RJ said. "He might say something to somebody else and they might tell me."

RJ stopped talking. He couldn't believe how ashamed he was about what happened at the bowling alley.

"Well, if he does, you be sure not to get riled up again."

"I won't."

"I've got a plan: something that might get you out of this whole court mess."

"Really?!?" RJ suddenly felt a sense of relief he hadn't felt since the whole thing with Tim Craig happened. He moved back a bit more in his seat so he could make sure his grandpa wasn't pulling his leg. "What are you gonna do?"

"Well, this other boy isn't alone in what happened. So you started it, but he did provoke you. Now the way I figure it, this was just an event among two kids, opposites, that got out of hand. You shouldn't have tried to beat him up, but I'm thinking that you're gonna be on your best behavior now. So I'm gonna find out where this boy lives and I'm going to talk to his parents."

"You are?" He was still excited, but at the same time he knew he might look like a wuss if people thought he was using his grandfather to solve his problems. RJ may have changed, but he was still RJ Boynton; brother of Joel Boynton. He had a reputation to think about. "How?"

"I'm gonna look them up. Unless of course you know where he lives?"

RJ nodded his head. He couldn't remember how he knew where Tim lived but he did.

"Well then, we're halfway there. I figure we call them, make an appointment to meet with his father sometime in the evening, and we'll both talk to him. The man will see you, you can apologize, and this whole thing will hopefully be behind you."

"Yeah, I hope." RJ didn't really think this would work. If Tim Craig was a jerk, his dad was probably a jerk too. Why would he help RJ? He probably wanted the court to throw the book at him.

"But you better watch yourself. You're young now so you've got a lot of outs, but every day you get a little older, and you have to be that much more responsible. Also, there's gonna come a time when you're not gonna have your mother or I to help you. You could end up like Joel, which is exactly what I'm trying to avoid."

"Joel isn't bad," RJ offered. He respected his grandpa, but when push came to shove, he respected Joel a lot more. Plus, he didn't like hearing anybody say anything bad about his brother.

"Oh, he's not? You think they put you in jail because you've made the right choices?"

His grandpa stared at him. He didn't laugh after he said that. In fact, he didn't seem anything but angry.

"That boy has had chance after chance and he always ends up back in trouble. He's probably told you he never wants to go back there."

"He doesn't," RJ said sternly.

"That's where you're wrong. You don't want to steal from people, you don't steal."

"He said he didn't do it."

"Every criminal says that. You think there's anybody who lives where he lived that actually admits to being guilty of something? He'll go back, and you'll go there too, if you keep up with the way you were going."

"I don't want to go to jail."

"Well, then you won't ... but it all comes down to your choices. So far, at least since I've been here, you seem like you've made some good ones."

RJ didn't like thinking about members of his family being in jail. It was at moments like this that he really wished his dad was still around, Joel was living at home, and that his mom wasn't sick. At the same time, his grandpa probably wouldn't be living with him. RJ might be totally different, and there'd be no reason to have his grandpa there. They hadn't been together that long, but RJ was really glad they had gotten to know one another.

Chapter 15.

The winter day had been surprisingly warm, so RJ felt a little weird wearing Joel's old denim jacket around school. He didn't usually wear a jacket – even when it was pouring rain – so he knew that wearing one today would definitely have some kids wondering. Some of the teachers gave him weird looks and probably thought he was coming off a high of some sort. In fact, it wasn't until lunchtime, when Yogi and RJ were sitting in their spot, that Yogi asked about the cast that RJ was supposed to have given him.

"They threw it away," RJ explained.

"What?" Yogi genuinely seemed upset about not getting the piece of plaster that had been decaying on RJ's arm.

"Yogi, you wouldn't have wanted it anyway. It was all dirty and smelly from being on my arm. It was really gross, and when the doctor took it off he didn't even offer it to me; he just throw it in the trash."

"Well, I would have at least liked to have seen it."

"I'm sorry."

Yogi was sure acting different today. He never questioned RJ about anything. He couldn't understand why he was so upset.

"It's fine," Yogi offered. "It's just … my parents are talking about moving again."

"Oh…" RJ sighed, putting everything together. If Yogi's parents moved, that would mean that he would have to go to a new school. That would mean starting all over again somewhere else. Without RJ.

Despite being somebody that most people didn't talk to, Yogi had a certain status because of his friendship with RJ, the school time bomb. He hated to think of himself as that, especially now that his grandfather was starting to be everything that his father and mother weren't, but, like it or not, that is how people thought of him. A lot of kids didn't associate with him, teachers ignored him, and it was all based on who he was perceived to be.

    Yogi had already moved a bunch of times. Meanwhile, RJ hadn't ever been outside of his city. He thought when he got older he might want to leave, but with people leaving him throughout his life, he found that he just wanted something stable and familiar. Who cared if he didn't go anywhere? Where did RJ Boynton have to go?

    "I hope they don't decide to. They say they probably won't. My sister threw a fit when my dad said his company was thinking about it; she was crying and everything. Last time she threw a fit was when they wanted her to go to this dance with a family friend. She ended up not having to go."

    RJ laughed and Yogi smiled.

    Roger Rivera walked up to them. He had a look in his eyes, a mission, and something told RJ that Tim Craig was behind it. He had to play it cool, especially if his grandpa really did hope to get him off the hook with the whole court mess.

    "Hey RJ, I hear you got your cast off?" Roger stated.

    "Yup," RJ said. He then spat on the ground for no other reason than he thought it might let Roger know that he didn't think too much of him.

    "Tim Craig says he's gonna get you."

    "That wuss waited until I got my cast off?" RJ half laughed. He started to feel the anger again. He hated how easily people could push his buttons, and he hoped it would stop one day, but for now he felt helpless when people got under his skin and hurt his feelings.

    "He said he'd never fight you with that thing because you'd use it against him."

"Damn right I would: I'd break his face with it." He was really sounding like his old self now, "And then I'd throw him through a window."

Roger's expression completely changed after RJ said that. He probably had told Tim that he'd threaten RJ, figuring that with the court date and all of RJ's other problems, he wouldn't do anything to him. RJ had picked up on this. Something happened to him when he got mad. It was like he got smarter. Sadly, this was the only time when RJ felt that way. Roger had never acted scared of RJ, but he'd never been this bold either.

"I might break your face right now so Tim can see what's gonna happen if he ever talks about me behind my back again."

"Dude," Roger started, the color in his face quickly leaving his cheeks. "I was just telling you. So you know. I wasn't saying…" He was really starting to stammer now.

RJ eyed Yogi, whose lower jaw was dangling open, making him look scared like it always did. He started to stand up so he could get in Roger's face. Nobody came up and threatened him without at least some physical intimidation.

Then, out of nowhere, RJ started to remember some of what his grandfather said.

"You be sure not to get riled up again."

It was just like how he always thought about things Joel had told him when he got in fights. Still, RJ had to do something: he couldn't let anybody think he was just going to take a threat.

So he chose words instead.

"Tell Tim that I'm not afraid of him or his meathead brothers. Tell him that Joel is coming back to town and that he and his friends are gonna be after their whole family."

"Okay," Roger said, any boldness he had originally brought to the conversation now gone. "I gotta bail. See you later."

RJ glared at Roger as he walked away, his shoulders slouching. He looked so sad. Like he'd bitten off way more than he could chew, and now he had to go back and tell Tim that, court date or not, RJ Boynton was still as tough as ever. The more RJ stared at him, the more he realized he was starting to feel bad about making Roger feel that way.

He turned back to Yogi, who seemed to be at a loss for what to say to RJ. Whenever RJ threatened people, he noticed that Yogi always got scared as well.

"When is Joel coming back?" Yogi finally asked.

"Soon."

"Where's he gonna live?"

"He'll probably live at our house with my mom, my grandpa and me."

RJ began to recall how excited that prospect made him. A full house: people always around. It wouldn't last forever, but for RJ, it was better than nothing at all.

Aside from the run-in with Roger, things had been going too good for RJ. He knew that eventually he was going to get dinged for something. He was reading the second book in the Diary Of A Wimpy Kid series (RJ liked this book because the characters in it were so different than he was) when Mrs. Gonzales summoned him to talk with her at her desk. Even though RJ knew Mrs. Gonzalez liked him, she still had high expectations, so he was ready to get in trouble for something. As he walked to her desk, he tried to recall all of the tests and assignments he had recently turned in so he could have some sort of an excuse.

"What are you trying to do? Go to college or something?" Mrs. Gonzalez smirked. He just stared at her. "What's the matter? You got superglue in your mouth?"

RJ smiled after she said that. She was joking.

"No," he smiled cautiously.

"Then what's the meaning of this?"

Mrs. Gonzalez held up a math test RJ had taken. He didn't think he'd done that well on it, which was why at the top of the test he was surprised to see a big "B-."

B-...

That was the highest grade RJ had ever gotten on a math test. At least the highest he could remember.

"I got lucky, I guess." He was trying to play it cool, but inside he was about to burst. Maybe he wasn't so dumb after all?

"Well, you just keep getting lucky." Mrs. Gonzalez smiled. "I'm very pleased with the big improvement in your school work, RJ."

"Thanks," he offered.

"'Thanks,'" Mrs. Gonzalez said, imitating him. "Now we need to work on your social skills."

Mrs. Gonzalez handed him his test and RJ took it. He walked back to his desk and folded it as if the paper was no big deal. But it was, and RJ knew it. Maybe there really was something to all his grandpa's talk about getting a good education and walking the straight and narrow?

Later that evening, RJ was sitting in the living room with his grandfather as he watched the news on TV. RJ was doing his homework and was actually surprised that he was kind of enjoying it. He had fallen behind with his class as they were reading The Outsiders. He had to read a bunch of chapters and do a few reading comprehension assignments. The more he read the book, the more he related to the story of Ponyboy, Dallas, Johnny, Darry, Sodapop, Two-Bit and the rest of the characters. RJ wasn't sure he got everything in the book, but he figured he understood enough. He sort of saw himself like

Ponyboy. Yogi was a lot like Johnny. And RJ felt Joel was a lot more like Dallas than Darry or any of the other characters.

RJ was starting to find that if he did his homework in front of the TV (and he did it that way a lot more now), he didn't get too distracted.

His grandpa had been so happy about the B- on the math test that he had taken RJ out for some ice cream, and even made it a point to put his test on the fridge where anyone who came over could see it. When his mom came home from work she didn't see it right away, and his grandfather had to point it out to her. She was excited and gave RJ a big hug and a kiss, but sometimes RJ wondered if, when she did those things, she did them not because she wanted to, but because she thought she had to.

The phone rang and his mom picked it up.

"How are your studies coming?" his grandfather asked.

"Good," RJ said. "I'm almost done."

"That's what I like to see. We had an Uncle Bill who went to college but that was about it. Who knows? You keep up the hard work, stay good with your behavior, and you could be the next Boynton that goes."

College? RJ thought to himself. He was having a tough enough time in the 7th grade. He couldn't imagine what the coursework there would be like.

"So you never went?"

"Me?" His Grandfather laughed. "I didn't finish high school."

"Why not?"

"I didn't want to." His grandpa stared at him and quickly sought to quell the gears he could tell were turning in RJ's head. "But don't do what I did. I regret not getting my diploma. I was stupid. I thought I knew everything; didn't need to learn stuff. I wanted to have fun with my friends. I've spent every day since I dropped out realizing that you can't do that. I made a big mistake. I'd give almost anything to be able to go back, be your age, and do it all again. I don't know if I'd go to college. I'd like to, but I'm not sure I've got the head for it. I'd definitely finish high school, though."

RJ's mom walked into the room holding the cordless phone.

"RJ, your brother's on the phone." She held the phone out to him. RJ first noticed that she didn't look nearly as tired as usual. Then it sunk in what she said.

Joel...

JOEL WAS ON THE PHONE.

RJ's cool brother – the person who was talked about with reverence by all the kids in the town – he was calling to speak with him. No matter how big Joel got, no matter how cool he was, RJ would always be his brother. RJ stood up and took the phone from his mom.

"Hello?" he asked, noticing his grandfather staring at the TV, acting as if he hadn't even heard Joel's name being said. His mother sat on the couch where RJ had been.

"What's up, little man?" Joel asked, his voice deeper than RJ remembered it being. Through the phone receiver it sounded like there were a lot of things happening around him.

"Not much. Just hanging out ... I'm doing my homework, right now." RJ felt dumb for saying that. Joel wouldn't think much of homework.

"Homework? I didn't expect the kid who runs through glass doors to be doing that!" Joel laughed a little after he said that.

"You heard about that?"

"Yeah: Mom just told me. I can't wait to tell some of my friends about this. They already think you're cool. This'll just confirm it. You're becoming a legend, RJ. Just like me."

"Cool," RJ said, at the same time remembering what his grandpa had just said about school, college, and staying on the straight and narrow.

"So Mom has Grandpa living with you now?" Joel's tone was indifferent.

"Yeah."

"That sounds like fun." Joel laughed again. "I'd rather be locked up. Living with that guy would kill me."

RJ turned away so that his grandfather wouldn't know they were talking about him.

"He's not that bad."

"Mom said you were throwing a fit..."

"No," RJ said, interrupting his brother. The legend. "Maybe at first, but not now. He's been real nice to me."

RJ moved out of the living room and into his bedroom. For some reason, RJ thought his grandfather could hear Joel through the receiver. It didn't seem like these two had anything good to say about each other.

"I'm coming home soon and we're gonna raise hell," Joel said, changing the subject. "I think it might be time to get you drunk, little man."

"Really?" RJ had sipped beer with his dad a few times. He and Yogi had also stolen beer from the store and tried to split it. The taste was too much for them, and they ended up throwing it away. Then he remembered the big question he wanted to ask his brother. "Where are you? Are you still in Rittner?"

"Yeah. I'm staying with some friends. Rodney just came up to visit. He said he's gonna have a party for me when I come back to Bentonville. I'll come over, pick you up and take you to it."

"No way." RJ started to think about how cool it would be. When word got around school that he had gotten drunk with his brother and his friends, he'd be the coolest kid ever. Who cared if RJ didn't like the way beer tasted.

"Yeah…" Joel said, excited, as if he was thinking about how cool it would be to come back to his hometown. His stomping ground. "I should be down there soon. I'll call you before, so get ready, we're gonna rage. You're entering the big time now, brother."

If RJ had been excited before, he was really excited now. It was almost like he was a soldier in his brother's army and he was being promoted in rank.

"Why don't you come home now?" RJ asked.

"Business, RJ. I gotta be where I gotta be, you know? I'll be back soon." Before RJ could say anything, some loud music started up in the background. It sounded really loud through the receiver, so it must've been deafening where Joel was. "HEYYY!" he yelled to whoever was in the room. RJ then couldn't hear anything as his brother cupped the phone.

"Joel?" RJ asked. He started to get nervous. He hoped his brother wasn't getting in a fight or something.

"I gotta go, RJ. I'll talk to you soon."

"Okay, Joel…"

Before RJ could say anything else, his brother hung up the phone. He thought about calling him back, but when he checked the number on the caller ID all it said was: "Unavailable."

RJ walked back out into the living room. His grandpa was still watching the news: only now he was yelling at the TV.

"Of course that happens: the bastard's got no heart!" he stated loudly. He only just seemed to notice that RJ had walked back into the living room. "You done talking to that no good kid you call a brother?"

"He's not no good," RJ shot back. He was so quick, he surprised both his grandfather and himself.

"A person that doesn't care about anyone or anything, is no good. Period."

"How do you know what he cares about?" RJ was raising his voice now.

"Trust me. I know."

RJ's grandpa was so calm as he said that, he couldn't think of anything else to say. He talked to RJ about Joel in a way that suggested he knew something RJ didn't. Like maybe his grandpa used to not care about anything. RJ didn't want to argue, so he picked up his homework and finished it in his bedroom.

Chapter 16.

"Happy Birthday to you! Happy Birthday to you! Happy Birthday, to RJ! Happy Birthday to you!" his grandpa and mother sang as he brought over a small cake to the table. It had one candle and white frosting on it. It also said, "Happy Birthday RJ" in blue icing. His grandpa had sung more than his mom, but RJ wasn't going to let that bother him too much.

"Well, aren't you going to make a wish? Or are you so old now you can't blow out one candle?" RJ's grandpa laughed.

"I can do it," RJ said. He closed his eyes and took a deep breath. It had been awhile since he had really celebrated his birthday with an actual birthday cake. He was also torn about what he should wish for. RJ desperately wanted Joel to come home. He wanted his mom to no longer be sick. He wanted his grandpa to keep living with them. Since he didn't have a lot of time to choose, RJ quickly wished for all of those things to happen.

No sooner had RJ blown out the candles then his mom started to cough. She stood up and patted RJ's head.

"Happy Birthday, baby," she said and left the room.

RJ stared at the cake. For some reason, he felt weird about looking at his grandpa. As if he knew something about RJ that nobody else knew. Like how much his mom not being there bothered him. He couldn't help wondering: if she wasn't sick, if she wasn't so tired all the time, would she be any more involved with him than she was?

"She got you this," his grandfather said, handing him a wrapped package. By its size and shape, RJ could tell that it was a video game. RJ's grandfather also handed him a card. "That's from me."

RJ put the video game down.

"Should I open it now?" RJ asked.

"Well, that depends. I personally don't like getting gifts. There's something about people making a fuss about me that gets me all uptight. I like giving them, so I guess it just depends on how you feel about being on the receiving end."

"I'll open it," RJ said.

At first he started to try and open it without ripping the envelope. That resulted in a small paper cut, so he just ripped it open. The card had a picture of a ship at sea. The words "To A Great Grandson" were embossed on it. RJ opened up the card itself. It said something about sailing into the future, but RJ was more concerned with what his grandpa actually wrote. It said:

Russell,

You are a great grandson and a great friend. There's nothing you can't do.

Love,

Grandpa

"Look, why don't you just start counting the money. That's what you really care about anyway." His grandpa laughed.

"No, it isn't." RJ said.

"Well, just know that I meant what I wrote. Also, don't go spending all that loot in one place. I imagine at your age that should hold you over for awhile. I'm gonna get a couple of plates for the cake."

RJ's grandfather went into the kitchen to get some plates and forks. RJ reread what he wrote and only then seemed to notice the money that his grandfather spoke of. It was two twenties and one ten dollar bill.

Fifty bucks!

RJ had never been given this much money at one time in his life. Kids like Tim Craig and even Yogi probably got it for their birthdays all the time. For RJ, it was like he was rich.

"Thank you," he said.

"Not a problem. It's my pleasure. It also wouldn't kill you to put some of that in the bank." RJ must've made a face because his grandpa quickly said, "Or, you could just buy some games."

His grandpa walked over with two forks, two plates, and a large knife. He started cutting the cake and, just as he'd hoped, his grandpa cut them both two very large pieces. RJ's birthday may not have been some major event, and it wasn't necessarily the kind of birthday a kid dreams about having, but it was just fine by him. It had been a long time since his special day felt this special.

Chapter 17.

As RJ and his grandpa sat on the bus, he noticed that his arm was hurting him. He didn't know why but he did know that he hadn't been this nervous since the day the whole mess with Tim Craig started.

And this was exactly who RJ was going to see. Sort of.

After telling him that he was going to talk to Tim's father on his behalf, RJ's grandfather had actually set up a meeting with Mr. Craig. It hadn't been easy, his grandpa said, as Tim's dad was "hell bent" on seeing RJ prosecuted, but somehow RJ's grandfather had at least managed to get them in the door. Which was why on a hot Thursday after school, RJ was wearing his best button shirt and jeans (his grandpa was wearing a button shirt and slacks) and taking a bus trip to the home of Tim Craig.

"My arm hurts," RJ said.

"Makes sense," his grandpa started. "It shrunk while it was in the cast. It's growing again. You've never heard of growing pains?"

He noticed that his grandfather seemed a little on edge today. Even though he had set up the talk with Tim Craig's father, RJ figured he was starting to get nervous about what he was going to say? Then RJ realized they were both nervous about the same thing ... letting the other one down.

"Yeah," RJ offered.

"Well, that's what's probably happening." His grandfather seemed to be going out of his way to not look at him.

For a brief moment, RJ half hoped that he would change his mind about this talk. There were so many ways it could go wrong. RJ honestly didn't think Tim's dad was going to let him off the hook, so what was the point? He hated that he and his grandpa had to go over there like they were looking for charity.

He'd rather be sent to juvenile hall. He'd rather have anything happen to him if that meant not giving Tim something to hold over his head. He started to imagine the talk going really bad. RJ might get upset ... there was no might about it: he would get upset. What if his grandfather lost his temper? What if another fight broke out? What if the cops had to be called?

RJ decided to stop thinking about all of this. He needed to be positive. He was soothed by the fact that if this worked, he'd be saving his mom and his grandpa a whole lot of trouble.

Who cared if he didn't look tough or cool? Who cared if Tim Craig and his friends made fun of him? They would always make fun of him. Maybe not to his face, but they would do it just the same, so what did it matter?

RJ was starting to feel better. If things went well ... he would basically be getting a second chance. He could continue doing well in school, his big brother Joel would come live with them, he'd get along with their grandfather, maybe go to a trade school, RJ's mom would get better...

The bus came to their stop.

"Let's go." His grandpa stood up quickly and started getting off the bus.

RJ followed him off the bus and then down the street. His grandpa took out a piece of paper with the directions to the Craig house on it. For some reason, RJ had a feeling that, after today, he'd never forget how to get there.

"These people have money, that's for sure," his grandfather commented as they looked at the houses on Tim Craig's block.

RJ looked around, taking in just how much better the homes in Tim Craig's part of town were compared to where he lived. The homes by Tim Craig were newer and bigger. It seemed like the roads were repainted every month and the lawns were always kept up. RJ had once heard that it was a law that the people who lived in Tim's tract had to make their homes look a certain way.

"Yeah, Tim is always bragging about how rich his family is," RJ said.

"That's probably the beginning and the end of why you two don't like each other. The haves and the have nots. Been that way since the Bible was written."

"I have stuff."

"Yeah, but there's always somebody who has more, and believe me, they'll tell you about it."

RJ didn't say anything. He knew his grandpa wasn't trying to make fun of him, but it still bothered him a little to think that even his own grandfather would notice how much more Tim Craig had than him.

He then started to wonder what he'd done to get so little? RJ would give anything to live in a place this nice, and that was what really hurt him. As much as he disliked Tim Craig, he really did want what he had. Why a jerk like him got a big house and two parents was beyond him, but that seemed to be the way things always worked out for RJ. Someday he would have his own house. He'd have a good job (courtesy of all that hard work in school). He'd have a family, and it would all be in a neighborhood like this.

"14702: this is it," his grandfather said, breaking into his thoughts.

"We're here?" RJ asked, suddenly realizing that this talk with Tim Craig's dad was about to happen.

"Yup." His grandfather turned toward him and began to fix up RJ's clothes. "You look presentable. How do I look?"

RJ looked at his grandpa's tired, wrinkly face, his beard, his worn clothing … and he saw himself again. Suddenly he started to get choked up. He brushed the lint off his grandfather's jacket.

"You look good," RJ said in a low voice.

"Okay then." His grandpa fixed a stare on him and put both hands on RJ's shoulders. "Let's get this done."

He turned and walked toward the front door of the Craig House. RJ followed him.

Tim's house was really nice inside. There were no toys, video games, papers, unread mail or clothes littered all over the floor. The furniture wasn't brand new, but it wasn't old and falling apart like it was at RJ's house. There were bookshelves full of all kinds of books, and as RJ and his grandfather sat in Tim Craig's father's office, RJ couldn't take his eyes off all the baseball memorabilia he had. There were pictures of Mr. Craig with a bunch of players RJ didn't know the names of, small autographed bats, autographed pennants, etc. He even had pictures of himself playing the game at different ages. There were also pictures of Mr. Craig with people RJ assumed were family members. His dad, his brothers, his brother's children. RJ's grandpa had been quick to pick up on all the baseball stuff, and that was what they were discussing.

"Yeah, I do like the game of baseball," RJ's grandfather said. RJ noticed he was being a lot more outgoing than normal.

"I had a great time playing in college. It was a lot of fun," Mr. Craig said. He was somewhat overweight, with a nicely groomed beard. He struck RJ as the type that, even in a T-shirt and jeans would look dressed up. "So … let's get down to business."

"Yessir," RJ's grandpa stated enthusiastically. "That's why we're here: to get this whole mess behind us."

"Uh-huh," Tim's dad said, shooting RJ a look. It was quick – almost dismissive – and it made RJ bristle a bit, but he decided not to let it bother him. Not only did he want the reason he was there to work out, but he wanted to make his grandfather proud.

"It seems they had a bit of a fight, and both of them ended up getting hurt," his grandpa offered.

"He could've killed my son," Mr. Craig said quickly. "He attacked him in a bathroom. Had there not been an adult in there to stop him, I'm scared to think about what might've happened."

"I can understand that," RJ's grandfather said, and for a moment RJ got really scared. He sounded nervous. The man who had come here to talk on RJ's behalf was scared. If this was the case, they were done.

Tim Craig's dad turned and looked at RJ.

"Do you understand what you did?" His voice was getting louder. As if he'd been waiting to lay into RJ on behalf of his son.

"Yes, sir." RJ's voice sounded very strange to him. It probably had something to do with the lump of fear in his throat.

"Do you realize how badly you could've hurt my son? He says you're always picking fights with him..."

"That's not true!" RJ said loudly.

"RJ," his grandpa said, putting his hand on him.

"Tim always picks on me too!! You know that, grandpa. He makes fun of my mom ... who's sick. He's always talking about how much money he has. He makes fun of my clothes...." Tears started to form in his eyes and RJ tried to continue talking, but he couldn't. If he did, he was going to start bawling, and he didn't want to do that. It wasn't just that he didn't want to give the Craigs the satisfaction of making him cry ... he didn't want to blow it any more by not listening to his grandfather. He believed in RJ.

"I'm sorry," he managed to say as his emotions subsided a bit. A few warm tears burned as they rolled down his cheeks, but there were only a few. "About everything."

He wiped the tears from his face and looked at Mr. Craig for a second. While he still seemed to be looking down at RJ, something in his eyes seemed to say that he believed him. Maybe he even understood why RJ wouldn't like his son.

There was silence in the room.

For a brief moment, RJ thought about his mom, his grandpa, Joel, his father, and that was all it took. He started to cry a lot ... he couldn't help it. RJ was thinking of everything now. The thought of having to leave his house – of going who knows where – was too much for him. He was trying to stop, but that made him cry even more. Eventually, he started sobbing and just seemed to be grasping for air which, for the moment, was better than crying.

"So what do you propose?" Tim's Dad finally said. He offered RJ a tissue from a gold-colored box on his desk.

RJ took one of the tissues and wiped his eyes and nose. He wanted to blow it, but the tissue was too wet to do that.

"Well," his grandfather started, his voice sounding a little more confident, as if he was finally getting a chance to say something he'd wanted to say his whole life. "We can't pay you anything because we can barely pay our own bills. The boy is right: his mom is sick, his dad is dead, and his brother's in and out of jail. Even if his dad was here, it wouldn't matter: he was no good, just like his son. I imagine if I was RJ's age, and my mom was in a bad way, and somebody said something about her, I think I probably would've reacted the same way. I don't know about your upbringing, and this certainly doesn't make it right, but this kid was born into a family where he never had much of a chance."

RJ's grandpa looked at Tim's dad for a moment.

"Since he could walk, RJ's been running around, causing trouble. Since he could talk, he's had a big mouth. I'm not perfect, Mr. Craig. I was an alcoholic for most of my life ... I am an alcoholic; and aside from RJ and his mom, I've got no family to speak of. When she told me about what happened with your son, I was flat broke with literally nowhere to go."

He looked back at Tim Craig's father, and then seemed to focus his attention to something on his desk. That seemed to help him organize his thoughts.

"She probably didn't want me coming to live with her. I wasn't much of a dad and I don't figure I'm much better now. But ... I've got some life experience, and I know that if I could stop myself from making certain mistakes, I would. I've gotten to know this kid a bit over the past few months, and based on what I've seen, I think he deserves another chance. I think he's seen too much bad in his life. He's seen where all that stuff can lead you."

RJ's grandfather then looked directly into Mr. Craig's eyes. RJ noticed that they too were filling up with tears. He had never seen a person that old even come close to crying.

"So you can press charges against him; he attacked your son. That's your right. And we'll have a court date, and RJ'll most likely be sent to juvenile hall. If I was in your position and someone did what he did to my kid, I'd be mad."

He then turned and looked RJ dead in the eyes.

"Look at him ... he's a baby. He's just learning how the world works ... but he sadly has an unfortunate education a lot of other boys didn't get. One they would never want."

RJ's grandpa cleared his throat and looked back at Tim Craig's dad.

"So he'll go to juvenile hall, he'll get out in a few months, and maybe he'll get back on track. Then again, maybe he won't. The point I'm making is that this court thing is going to leave a mark. A permanent mark that will be on RJ for the rest of his life. It might be small and maybe he'll learn from it, but it's still a mark, and I'd like to see somebody give him more of a chance."

His grandfather had done it. Tim Craig's father agreed to drop the charges which would cancel RJ's sentencing date. This whole mess – at least the part of it that might see RJ get sent away – was now behind him. He was so excited he practically ran out of the Craig house. He had also been really excited that Tim Craig hadn't been home when he was there. His dad would no doubt tell him how RJ started crying (he might even say that his grandpa almost did as well), but RJ didn't care about that. He had been given a second chance when he really needed it.

One of RJ's biggest fears was that Mr. Craig was going to sit RJ and Tim down side by side and have them recount everything each of them had ever said to one another. In RJ's mind, Tim would no doubt keep his cool while he blew his top and was taken away for the rest of his life.

"Slow down," his grandfather kept saying as they walked down the street. RJ had tried to remind himself to not walk as fast, but he was filled with so much energy he just wanted to jump around.

He'd been cleared.

His grandpa had managed to talk RJ out of a major problem. Now, all RJ had to do was keep doing good, not let his temper get the better of him, not let himself be set off, and he'd be okay.

"Well, we did it," RJ's grandpa said as they sat down at the bus stop. He looked tired, RJ noticed. The bus ride and all the walking and talking had probably taken a lot out of him.

"Yeah," RJ offered.

"I thought you almost blew it ... with all that blubbering," he said with a wink.

"I'm sorry about that."

"Don't be. It turns out it probably helped us. You start doing that in court, it may not help you. This way, Craig saves face. Gets to end this whole mess on his terms."

"So you think he wanted to drop the charges?" RJ couldn't imagine that.

"I don't know about that, but this way he doesn't have to deal with it anymore. Look at that place he has. You said that Tim has two brothers. He probably has some pets as well; cars. That kind of lifestyle doesn't come cheap. You work so hard it probably gets hard to enjoy it all. You always gotta work to keep it up. Dropping those charges, now he's got less things on his plate." His grandfather took out a piece of gum and offered one to RJ. He took it, and they both sat silently for a moment chewing their gum together.

RJ nodded off a bit on the bus ride home, and when he got there he just went to his room and flopped down on the bed. Tim Craig's house was only a short bus ride away, but over the course of that afternoon RJ felt like he'd been to another world and back.

Chapter 18.

RJ's arm continued to bother him. He assumed it would start feeling better once his cast had been off for awhile. He figured it would go back to its regular size and he would never have pain again. Well, his arm had basically gone back to its regular size, but this didn't stop it from hurting here and there. The pain wasn't sharp – it was throbbing and dull mostly – but there were times when a sharp pain would jolt through it. This would happen if RJ carried something in a weird way, or if he reached for something at an angle. It wasn't bad enough to complain about, and he'd been taking care of himself long enough that he could take a few Tylenol if he needed to.

As RJ got dressed that morning, he decided not to think about his arm because today he was going to see Joel. After all this time, after a few letters and some phone calls, he was finally coming back to town. RJ wanted to look cool: as if he'd grown up since they'd last seen one another. It'd been almost two years and RJ felt like he'd grown up a lot, even though when he looked in the mirror he didn't really see any difference in how he looked physically.

He also thought that maybe he could help Joel. If he did stay at home, maybe he wouldn't be so quick to go out and get into trouble if he somehow felt responsible for RJ? If he realized, like RJ had, that his actions had an effect on more than just himself and whoever he was directing his anger at.

Joel had called RJ a few days before and given him the plan. Rodney was going to bring Joel into town around 1pm. They were going to come by the house, drop off some things, pick up RJ, and take him to his coming home party at Rodney's. RJ never really liked Rodney, but that was because Rodney always acted like he didn't want RJ around. RJ had always put up with it because he wanted to hang out with his brother, but they were 10 years different in age, so it wasn't like Joel was going to ditch him for RJ.

    Joel was going to be there in an hour and RJ had made sure to get up early, do his chores (which required him to use the vacuum cleaner and get yelled at for "making too much damn noise, too early in the morning," by his grandpa), and he even got most of his homework done. It was Sunday, and RJ usually got his schoolwork done that evening. However, today he didn't know how long or how late he was going to be out with Joel, and he didn't want to chance not getting it done. RJ had always wanted to be good, but he never felt like he had anybody to be good for. Things were different now.

    So RJ put some gel in his hair and combed it in a way that seemed cool. It was parted to the side, and RJ combed the front up and then back a bit. He didn't know why he combed his hair this way; he just seemed to remember liking the way it looked. As he stared at himself in the mirror, he suddenly realized who else combed their hair this way.

    His dad.

    Standing in the bathroom in Joel's worn denim jacket and a pair of jeans, he realized how much he looked like his father. Though RJ never got to know him that well, he had seen some pictures. In fact, when he was younger he used to stare at them, and now it was all coming back out as he got ready for his brother's welcome home party. He continued to stare at himself and felt really good about the way he looked. This wasn't something that RJ usually thought about, but now that he was, he wondered why he didn't think about it more. How could he present himself in dirty clothes and uncombed hair? How could he not take a shower at least three to four times a week? He decided that how he looked was going to be the next thing that he worked on.

    The clock in the bathroom said that it was 12:15pm.

RJ's grandpa was in the living room watching baseball. His mom was in the kitchen making lunch and talking on the phone. RJ walked over to the couch and sat down.

"You must have a pretty hot date!" his grandfather stated.

"Joel's coming today."

"Oh..." His grandpa got his usual angry look on his face when RJ mentioned his brother. "He planning on sticking around?"

"We're going to a coming home party for him at his friend Rodney's." RJ suddenly felt that his grandfather might feel left out. "You want to come?"

"Nah. I've got better things to do then celebrate the homecoming of someone who's just heading back to where he's been."

"He's not going back to jail," RJ offered, upset that his grandfather seemed intent on ruining something RJ had been looking forward to.

"He's not? This wasn't the first time he went there, you know."

"Yeah, but he said he learned his lesson this time..."

"He wasn't doing anything wrong," his grandpa interrupted. "He wasn't doing anything wrong the first time either. RJ, you hang out with enough criminals, and I have, you'll realize that they're all innocent until they're guilty."

They sat there for awhile in an uncomfortable silence. RJ's grandfather was moody, but today there was something else bothering him. Normally, there was a point to his snarky comments. A lesson that his grandpa was trying to put across to make RJ understand why he was so surly. RJ wasn't a stupid kid: he knew he'd passed the point of tender loving care with most people. He'd never get the love and affection that Tim Craig, or even Yogi, got from his parents. He didn't have people looking out for him, so he had to look out for himself.

And he did, the best he could, but too many times he hadn't done good enough. Now he had his grandfather here and there was some semblance of help. A sounding board with which RJ could decide if he was making choices that were right or wrong. Somewhere deep inside of him, he knew that Joel may not really be there for him, and even if he was, he wasn't the voice that RJ should be listening to.

RJ was playing his XBox when he looked at the clock and saw that it was 2:47pm. Joel was almost 2 hours late.

Maybe he had a lot of traffic coming from Rittner? Maybe Rodney's car had broken down?

Normally, RJ would be content to just hang out and play video games all day, but since he had started doing better in school, he was reading a lot more. Sure, it was only his assignments, but that was better than nothing, and it was a major improvement over not reading at all. The problem today was he didn't feel like doing that. More importantly, he wasn't supposed to be doing that today. He wanted to get something to drink from the kitchen, but he didn't want to see his grandpa and give him a chance to say any more bad things about Joel. He'd discretely made himself a sandwich and smuggled it into his room.

So RJ just kept playing Call of Duty and hoped that, any minute now, Joel would prove his grandfather wrong and come strolling through the front door like the neighborhood hero he was. Even a phone call now would be enough. The only problem was, RJ was starting to doubt that anything would happen.

At 4 o'clock, RJ made a decision. He was going over to Rodney's house. He had been there a few times with Joel so he knew where he lived. RJ had $120 in his piggy bank. He knew that $20 would be more than enough to get him there and back. Remembering how he'd gotten there when Joel drove him, RJ figured that he'd have to take at least 2 busses. If Joel was there, then he could give him a ride home because that was most likely (RJ still hoped) where he would be staying tonight.

    Once RJ decided that this was what he was going to do, he put on his jacket and left the house. He didn't figure there was any reason to tell his mom or his grandfather. If he did, they'd probably try and talk him out of going, and RJ's mind was made up. If Joel showed up and RJ wasn't there, chances were he'd just go to Rodney's anyway. RJ walked a few blocks and sat down next to a Mexican lady at the bus stop. The Mexican lady had a little girl with her, and she kept staring at RJ.

    He started thinking about everything that his grandpa had said, and RJ got a bad feeling throughout his body. Joel just might be what his grandfather said he was. If that was true, then all his brother would be was just another person in a long line of people that didn't care about RJ.

    All these thoughts were too much for him and RJ stood up, glared at the little Mexican girl and her mom now that they were both staring at him, and started walking again. He figured that he'd walk until he reached the street where he was supposed to change busses.

    The bus never came, and RJ found that his right leg was hurting him as he rounded the cul-de-sac to the house that Rodney lived in with his dad. RJ's arm, which hadn't been hurting him, was now bothering him again. According to Joel, Rodney had it easy because his dad drove a truck and was never home. That probably accounted for why Joel spent so much time over there when he used to live with RJ and his mom. RJ thought about living alone and then quickly stopped. He'd rather have a home full of people that acted like Tim

Craig than ever be alone. Rodney's house was a small, ranch style place, similar to RJ's. It too needed a new coat of paint and someone who worked on the grass regularly.

    As RJ walked up, he saw a few people outside. He heard music coming from the backyard and heard more people's voices. Instead of going through the front door, he walked through the side gate, which was hanging open. As he walked along the side of the house, RJ heard a more distinct mix of girl and guy voices. Then he thought of something...

    He was probably going to be the only "kid" at this party. Normally he didn't care too much (at least he didn't when he was younger), because when he came to a party he was coming with Joel. Even though today was supposed to be for RJ and his brother, RJ once again felt like an outsider. As if he was intruding on people or being a burden at something he was invited to. His arm started to hurt a little bit, and RJ started to think about leaving before anybody really saw him. Joel had to come home sometime, right? They could certainly hang out then, and RJ would have his brother all to himself.

    There were about 10 people in the small backyard. They were sitting around talking, drinking and smoking. A barbecue was cooking hamburgers, but there was nobody in front of it to make sure that they weren't burning. Some fast music was playing that nobody seemed to be paying attention to.

    "Little man!" RJ heard Rodney say. He looked in the direction of the voice and saw Rodney standing by the sliding glass door holding a beer. He didn't smile or anything. Rodney just stared at RJ, almost as if he was making sure that this was him, as it had been a long time since they had seen each other.

    "Hey Rodney," RJ said as he slowly walked over to him. "Is Joel here?"

"Yeah," Rodney said, half smiling, and then, almost as if to drive home the point of his brother not coming to see him, he added, "he's been here since last night."

Last night? RJ thought. Why did he come here and not to his own family? Maybe he came in too late? Maybe he was weirded out by his grandpa being there so he was picking his moment to come home?

"Where is he?" RJ asked eagerly.

"Now? Oh, he's not here now. He said something about needing to meet with some people, so he took my car."

"Oh," RJ said. "He's missing his own party."

Rodney didn't say anything after RJ said that. In fact, the way Rodney looked around the backyard at everyone, this quite clearly let RJ know that this conversation was over. Rodney then punctuated this by walking away from him and going over to another group of people. Before RJ had only thought he might be alone at this party; now he was.

RJ hung around the party for 10 minutes and decided to leave. He figured Joel might have a lot of "business" with other people. He had to if he was gonna miss his own coming home party, right? For a brief moment, RJ entertained the idea that Joel had taken Rodney's car to come and get him, but he quickly dismissed that. Joel was someone who always had plans and things to do and RJ, like always, wasn't a part of them.

Tired, he waited at the bus stop for one that would drop him near his house. RJ had thought about walking the whole way, but he was beat. He also didn't see any need to hurry home and hear his grandpa talk about how right he'd been. Still, despite all of this, RJ held out a small hope that in some way Joel would prove to be the brother/hero RJ remembered he was.

Chapter 19.

If there had been another way into the house besides the front door, RJ would have taken it. He thought about going through the back way, but the sliding door was always locked, and he didn't know how to remove the screen from his open bedroom window.

After everything that his grandfather had said about his brother, RJ was slowly resigning himself to the fact that maybe there was a decent amount of truth in it. He wasn't mad at Joel; just disappointed. When he was in jail, RJ could deal with being an afterthought in his life because Joel was away from everyone. He had been sure that, once his brother was released, he would come home and be a part of his life. Wouldn't he want to be around RJ and his mom after being away from them for so long?

The other thing bothering RJ was what people would think. His brother came home and didn't even see him. He was Joel's little brother. Joel was the coolest kid in the neighborhood, and when he was gone RJ sort of felt like he had inherited that role. Who cared if RJ wasn't as smart, or as popular as Joel? Joel was his brother, so RJ had to have some of that in him, didn't he?

As much as RJ hated to admit it, he never felt like people saw him that way. He knew he was cool and tough, but people didn't respect him. They feared RJ. Or worse, they ignored him altogether. So many times when RJ was around a lot of people, he felt like he wasn't there. His mother, his dead father, his teachers, his classmates ... everyone except for his grandpa had treated him that way. He was the only person who seemed to take an interest in RJ. So, of course he was trying to avoid him now, because he didn't want him to see what everyone else already saw.

104.

    Resigned, RJ walked inside hoping nobody would be in the living room and then he could just go into the bedroom and sleep. The only problem was, the day was just starting to end and RJ, who'd been saving his appetite for the party, hadn't eaten, and he was starving. He thought about tapping into the "Joel fund" and getting something to eat at Mike's Burgers around the corner, but he decided not to.

    As soon as he got inside, he found his grandfather watching a black and white movie on TV. RJ's mom walked out from the kitchen area holding a glass of water.

    "Where's Joel?" she asked.

    RJ stammered for a moment and tried to think of something to say. As he got older, he found that it was harder to lie than it had been when he was a kid. He thought it would be the opposite because he was smarter. Now, it was like he knew too much and couldn't make himself believe that people would believe what he was saying.

    "He's at Rodney's," RJ said, which wasn't a complete lie.

    "He didn't come back with you?"

    RJ subtly looked at his grandpa, who shook his head as he kept watching the movie.

    "Rodney said he got here last night." RJ saw his mother's face drop noticeably after he said that. She, like everybody in their family, didn't show too many emotions (except when RJ got in trouble), but when she did it really surprised him. Considering how good he'd been lately, he really hadn't seen anything from her in quite some time. She did smile and "Thank God" when she heard that her father had gotten him off the hook with Tim Craig.

    Without saying anything, RJ's mom turned and walked back into the kitchen to resume cooking. RJ looked at his grandfather, who was still watching the movie. Slowly, he walked into his room, closed the door, dropped face first onto his bed, and started to cry. A lot.

When RJ woke up, he wasn't sure how long he'd been asleep, but he had an awful headache. Trying to cry softly had taken its toll on him and he'd nodded off. He expected his pillow to be soaked with tears, but it wasn't, so he must've been out long enough for it to dry. He'd been having a hard sleep, not dreaming about anything, when he heard somebody knocking on his door.
"Yeah?" RJ asked.
The door creaked open and his grandpa stood there. The look on his face let RJ know that his grandfather knew he'd been crying.
"Were you sleeping?" his grandpa asked.
"Yeah, I'm tired. I walked a lot today."
"Oh. Then I guess you don't want to go to the movies."
The movies. At that moment, that was exactly where RJ wanted to be. To sit in a dark theater, be anonymous, and not have to think about anything other than what was happening on the screen.
"Yeah, they got a horror show playing at 8:30. I figure we eat what your mom is cooking and then we go."
RJ sat up and rubbed his eyes.
"Okay."
His grandfather turned and walked out of the bedroom.
"Why don't you get yourself together and come to the table?"
RJ got up off the bed and walked out of his room and into the bathroom across the hall. He turned on the light and looked at himself in the mirror. He thought he looked good in his old denim jacket and blue jeans. It had been a hot day, and walking around in jeans for a few miles wasn't all that comfortable. He

had sweat a lot, and being out in the sun had also made him tired. This, however, wasn't the reason he felt so old today. He started to think of all the kids his age that were just allowed to be kids. RJ caught himself before he really started thinking about all of this, because he knew that those thoughts would make him start crying again. He took one final look in the mirror, turned off the light, and walked out of the bathroom.

The bus dropped RJ and his grandpa off about half a mile from the theater. His legs hurt a little because of how much he'd already walked that day, but he didn't say anything. On the way there, they stopped at a dollar store to buy some candy. RJ liked that his grandfather thought the prices in the theater were too expensive, so that's why he loaded up on stuff before going inside. He also liked smuggling food into the theater and then waiting until the lights were low to open them up. RJ didn't think anybody would care if they were seen opening up food when the lights were on, but for him and his grandpa it was all part of the fun.

As they sat in the theater waiting for Scream 4 to start, his grandfather finally brought it up.

"So Joel was a no show?" he asked, knowing full well that he was.

"Yeah," RJ said. He started to think of something else to say – maybe a way to make it seem like Joel hadn't done what he did – but he stopped.

"Well Russell, I don't usually say 'I told you so,' because people are usually in such a bad way I don't want to make them feel worse. However, in this instance, for your own good, I've got to say it. I told you that Joel was no good and I knew he wasn't gonna show up. The thing is, he will come home. Probably when he's busted broke and has nowhere else to go, and that's because that's how people like him are. And I know this might be hard to understand because he's older than you, but people like yourself need to be stronger than that." His grandpa looked around the theater a bit.

"People like me?" RJ asked. He thought he knew what his grandfather meant, but he wasn't sure and he wanted to be. He was pretty positive that this was important.

"You're a good boy. You've got everything in front of you ... your whole life. You can do great things. Don't make the mistakes Joel did. It might seem cool and fun; much more fun than keeping up with school and staying out of trouble. And it is fun, that life that your brother lives, but it gets old quick, and when that happens you're older and it gets harder to make a good start for yourself. You're the kind of person that's smart enough to have a good life."

"Yeah," RJ said, letting his grandfather's words sink in. As he looked around the theater, RJ started to feel something really strange. He felt emboldened, like he was actually going to have a different life than he thought he was going to have. He was the kind of person who was smart, who could have a good life. The more he thought about it, the more RJ actually felt glad that Joel hadn't been there today. That he had the opportunity to go home and go to the movies with his grandpa.

Chapter 20.

A week passed and still no word from Joel. RJ had managed to give him the benefit of the doubt for the first couple of days. This was Joel Boynton. It made sense that this hometown hero might take awhile to come through. By day three, however, RJ found that he was back to business as usual. When he did think about his brother, he had to remind himself that he was no longer far away. So when Yogi came over that afternoon and suggested they go to the mall, RJ didn't think for a second that he might miss his brother if he happened to come over. By now, RJ assumed that he wouldn't, and if he did ... he'd deal with it then.

Aside from hanging out with Yogi, RJ had a purpose for going to the mall. He still had $114 in his piggy bank. Originally, that money had been for Joel's return, but now RJ was going to use $30 of it to buy his grandpa a present. RJ didn't quite know what he was going to buy, but he figured getting him a gift was a good thing. He had truly come to appreciate his presence in the house. It hadn't been too long ago that RJ couldn't stand the sight of that old man, with his snarky comments and idiosyncrasies. The way he seemed to talk down to RJ anytime he got the chance.

However, time had passed and RJ realized that his grandfather was tough on him because he cared. And RJ in turn had come to understand how much he cared about him. So, he figured that this gift would make him happy, and it would show his grandpa not only how much he cared, but how much different RJ was from the boy who had crashed through the glass door of the bowling alley.

As RJ and Yogi walked to the mall, RJ sensed that something wasn't right with his best friend. Yogi seemed preoccupied with other thoughts. This didn't bother RJ, but Yogi never seemed this zoned out about anything.

"You think $30 is enough to buy a good gift?" RJ asked.

"I don't know ... maybe?" Yogi looked at the ground.

"What would you buy your grandfather?" RJ already had some ideas for what he should buy his: A book, a jacket, something for the living room he slept in.... He was hoping that questions like this would snap Yogi out of whatever was on his mind.

"What does he like?" Yogi still stared at the ground; listless.

"Yogi!" RJ started, not realizing that he was really starting to get angry. "Stop answering my questions with a question! If you don't want to hang out, that's fine, but don't say you do and then not talk."

Yogi stared at him, and for a split second RJ thought his friend might hit him.

Yogi started crying instead. It wasn't small sobs either. It was the blubbering kind where Yogi's body started to shake.

"Yogi, what's the matter?" RJ asked. He was afraid people might see the two of them and think that RJ had hit him or something. "I didn't mean to make you cry."

"I know," Yogi said, wiping away his tears. "I'm just scared."

"What are you scared of?" RJ started to get the gears in his head turning. If someone had threatened or hurt Yogi, he considered them after him, too.

"I'm moving," Yogi finally said, and then he started crying harder.

"Really?" RJ's body went cold for a moment.

"My dad's job is transferring him to New Jersey. I don't want to go, but there's nothing I can do. He says we might come back in a year, but I doubt it. He always says that when we move."

All this time, RJ had thought that Yogi needed him. That somehow his parents knew how important their friendship was. He had made him cool. He'd been Yogi's best friend forever, and now all that was going away.

"When are you leaving?" RJ finally asked.

"In the summer." Yogi's tears had stopped a bit. "I'm sorry for being a crybaby."

"It's fine. There's nothing you can do ... that's what sucks."

"Yeah, I wish I could stay here. I'm gonna have to make all new friends."

Friends? RJ wondered. Didn't he mean friend?

"You will." RJ hoped he didn't sound as sad as he felt.

"You're so lucky, RJ."

"How am I lucky?" he asked incredulously.

"You don't care about anything."

RJ thought about telling Yogi he was wrong. That he cared about his mom, his grandpa, Joel, him.... Instead, RJ decided not to say anything. He was too mixed up because, again, his world was changing without him having any say about it.

He didn't care. That's what everybody thought about him. Even his best friend. That's what Yogi was, but RJ figured if he was going to be leaving (and it wasn't supposed to matter to him), he may as well get used to it now. What was the point of trying to change Yogi's mind about who he was? What was the point of being angry at his parents for taking him away from RJ? RJ knew that at his age he could never win against adults. He could fight with them, he could make things difficult for them, but he could never truly beat them. Not now.

RJ started to feel really sad. No matter what way he tried to think about it, no matter how close he was to him, Yogi was just going to be another person who was no longer a part of his life. It felt like all the time they had spent together didn't matter at all. Sure, they'd hang out until he left, and they'd probably even stay in contact for a bit, but like everything else, that would soon fade away until he and Yogi were strangers, just like they had been when they first met.

    Yogi was going someplace ... and as usual, RJ wasn't going anywhere.

    The bookstore had been uneventful and not as interesting or fun as RJ had hoped it would be. He rarely bought things (he rarely had money, and what he had, he didn't spend), so when he did, he liked to take his time. He window-shopped all the time, looking at various things he couldn't afford like video games, toys, and sometimes even clothes. Yogi was following after him like normal now. He was asking questions, talking about books RJ might want, and RJ noticed that his lisp was less pronounced.

    Everything seems normal, but it isn't, RJ reminded himself. It won't be long before I'm walking in this store ... before I'm walking in every store and Yogi isn't with me.

    After going back and forth on the kind of book RJ thought his grandpa might want, RJ found a $20 book on photography. It was a big book, too, and for $20 he figured it was probably good. It had a lot of pictures, and RJ hoped his grandfather liked it. He also thought that his grandpa could read it while RJ did his homework. He reminded himself to take the "Bargain Book" sticker off of it before he gave it to him.

    RJ had some money left over, so he asked Yogi if he wanted some ice cream. None of the kids ever seemed to give Yogi anything, RJ thought, so this might give him a good memory before he went away. He was also happy that he would be able to return $5 to his piggy bank after taking $30 from it.

    "I'm gonna get Mint Chip," Yogi declared.

    "I'm thinking I want Fudge Brownie," RJ said.

    "The chunks are too big. You don't get as much ice cream."

"Yeah, but it's filled with chocolate."

Yogi said something else, but RJ didn't hear him. His eyes had spotted Tim Craig and his brother Larry about 15 yards away on their bikes. His body went cold, and for a moment, his arm started to hurt. For some reason, RJ was too nervous to tell Yogi to cross the street.

He quickly remembered he was holding his grandfather's gift, and he handed it to Yogi.

"Run home," he stated.

"What?" Yogi asked, oblivious to the situation as he took it.

"GO HOME!" RJ yelled. "I'll get it later."

Yogi looked at RJ and then noticed Tim and Larry approaching. He stopped walking and looked at RJ, who smiled at Yogi as he turned away from him. RJ recalled how he had dodged a bullet a few months earlier when he had been out with Yogi and his grandpa. He wouldn't be so lucky today.

You can't dodge bullets forever, he thought.

"Hey look," Tim started as RJ stood about five feet from them. "It's the crybaby and his crybaby friend."

RJ stared at them. He realized that whatever had subsided between them since he and his grandfather had talked to Tim's dad was over. He honestly thought everything between them might be done, and from a legal standpoint it was, but that wasn't doing RJ any good now.

"You think it's cool to jump people?" Larry asked. He was the oldest of the Craig brothers – a senior in high school – and he was known for being both cool and tough. At one point him and Joel had been friendly, but RJ didn't figure that that would help his chances any. Man, what RJ wouldn't give for Joel to appear right now. To come out of nowhere like the hero in one of those western movies that his grandpa liked. The Boynton Brothers fighting together, beating the Craig Brothers all the way home…

That wasn't gonna happen today.

"This is between us," RJ said cooly. "You gonna always have your big brother fight your battles, Tim?"

"Hey." Larry laid his bike on the ground: all but ensuring RJ that they were gonna be the ones fighting. He moved closer to him.

"Joel's back, you know?" RJ said. "I hung out with him and Rodney yesterday."

He was lying, but Tim and Larry Craig didn't have to know that. Also, Larry's eyes had widened a bit and he wasn't advancing on Tim anymore, so what he said had worked for a moment.

"He's not here now." Larry lurched forward and pushed RJ.

"Are you gonna do something?" RJ asked, no longer thinking. He was just trying to remain composed. "Or are you gonna keep pushing a 13 year-old kid around?"

Larry genuinely seemed stumped by that question. Tim noticed this as well.

"Deck him, Larry! I'll kick his ass after that!!" he yelled.

Larry looked at his brother, annoyed.

"Yeah, hit me! Hit the little 13 year-old!" RJ yelled.

"Kill him, Larry!!" Tim was starting to get mad at his brother right now. "Kill him like HIS STUPID DYING MOM!!!!"

In that moment, that split second, RJ had all the advantage he was going to get in this fight. As Larry turned back to face him, RJ cracked him in the face. It wasn't his hardest punch, but it had been unexpected enough to both startle Larry and knock him off his feet. Before either of the Craig Brothers could realize what was happening, RJ turned toward Tim and punched him in the nose.

This was his best punch. The punch he'd been waiting to throw since Tim had started to pick on him. For a second, RJ's rage made everything go black; then he realized that he may have shattered Tim's nose. He was lying on the ground now, holding his face as blood poured down it and through his fingers.

RJ turned to tell Yogi to run but was then punched in the side of the head by Larry. The blow dazed RJ, but he still managed to get in a solid enough position to kick him in the balls. Instead of doubling over in pain, this only seemed to make Larry angrier. Before RJ could do anything, Larry punched him in the head again. Normally, this probably would have hurt him a lot more than it did, but he was so angry he couldn't focus on that. He tried to punch Larry in the throat, but he hit his chest instead. Larry got in another shot to RJ's head. RJ did his best to roll his head with it (like Joel had taught him), but his punches started coming so quickly that he couldn't dodge them all. He tried to reposition himself and get into his fighting groove, but it just wasn't possible today. The punches kept coming ... each one seemed harder and more accurate. Eventually, he stopped trying to throw punches and began to just cover up. RJ probably always would have lost to Larry Craig, he was so much bigger and stronger ... but he had gotten in some good shots on him. And he had hurt Tim, who was the one he really hated.

It wasn't long before RJ found himself on the ground. He had won a lot of fights, but he had also lost his share too, so he wasn't unfamiliar with what it felt like to lose once in awhile. Somehow Tim Craig had managed to get up, and RJ realized that his nose wasn't broken, and that this fight wasn't even close to being over. He figured both brothers were going to beat on him now. He tried to see if Yogi was still there, but he didn't want to expose himself too much. Even though he wasn't the same kid that ran through the glass door at the bowling alley, instincts kicked in and RJ curled himself into a ball as both Craig brothers wailed on him.

RJ wasn't sure how many punches and kicks he had taken; he just knew that some adult had seen him getting beaten up and they decided to stop it. RJ hadn't seen the person – he'd been too busy covering his face – but he had heard their voice, and they sounded like an older woman. After the brothers ran away, the woman bent down to see if RJ was okay. RJ didn't remember what he said to her. He just lay on the ground, his eyes closed, the fresh taste of blood in his mouth, and when he finally sat up he realized that Yogi was still there. He wasn't holding the gift RJ had bought for his grandpa.

Where's the gift? RJ thought to ask, but he soon discovered that his grandfather was talking to the lady that had saved him. She seemed to be describing what had happened as RJ's grandpa either nodded or shook his head. Yogi came over to him.

"Are you okay?" he asked. His lisp wasn't nearly as noticeable, which meant Yogi wasn't that nervous, so maybe RJ didn't look as bad on the outside as he felt?

"Yeah, I think," RJ started. "What did you do with the present?"

"I just left it in your house. When I got your grandpa."

"IS IT OUT? Did he see it?" RJ's head was starting to really hurt, and talking loud wasn't helping.

"I don't know. I didn't have time to put it in your room." Yogi's lisp was returning.

"It's cool. Thanks for getting him to help."

"Sorry I didn't help you, but you told me to run…"

"Yeah … I'm just glad his gift is okay."

RJ smiled at Yogi and then lay back on the ground. As he covered his eyes, he noticed that Yogi was staring at him curiously.

"What?" he asked, bringing his other arm under his head and resting it there.

"Well..." Yogi started, staring at RJ with an even more scrutinizing glare. "You have a black eye ... your nose is bleeding, and ... the side of your face looks scraped."

"Oh..." RJ would wear the marks of being in this fight for at least a couple of weeks. Still, it didn't sound like he'd been that badly banged up. Normally, it might bother him that he lost a fight.

Not today.

Today he just closed his eyes and let the sun shine on his bruised face. He even smiled a little bit. It had been two against one. He was starting to feel something very familiar, and it was making him feel really good. RJ had almost completely bought into all the things his grandfather had been talking about.

"Walking the straight and narrow," "Staying out of trouble," "Being a good person...." All of it.

He'd been fighting everything until he'd let his grandpa's words stick in his head. He actually thought he could have a normal, stable life. But with a mom who was too sick to care about him, a brother who didn't have time for him, a best friend who was leaving, and now Tim and Larry Craig had beat him up and most likely wouldn't get into trouble for it....

As much as RJ may have been trying to make himself believe otherwise, all along he'd probably known somewhere inside of him that what his grandfather spoke of was a sucker's game. The kinds of things you did if you weren't tough like RJ.

So as he lay on the hard concrete ground with his eyes closed, and his face and body busted up, his arm starting to throb again, RJ was quickly reminded of the person he'd been some months before when he crashed through the glass door at the bowling alley.

"Don't worry RJ," Yogi started. "Your brother or dad will get Tim Craig's family."

"No, they won't Yogi." RJ's head hurt so much he was starting to feel like he might throw up. "They aren't gonna do anything for me."

"Stop talking," Yogi said nervously. "You need to rest, RJ. You're not talking right."

Chapter 21.

RJ had had a lot of time to think about what had happened with Tim and Larry Craig. Three days' worth, as a matter of fact. Despite feeling alright after the fight, he had had a headache for the rest of Saturday and all day Sunday. Monday it subsided, but his grandfather told his mom that it might be a good idea for him to stay home "so the bruises could heal a little bit more." RJ had lain on the couch, half in and half out of consciousness, as he heard his grandpa console his mother, who seemed to sob the whole time.

"Why can't he just stay out of trouble?" she kept asking him.

His grandfather explained that this last time really wasn't RJ's fault. That Tim Craig and his brother had jumped him, and they could actually press charges against them now if they wanted to. He also said that since Tim Craig's dad had dropped the charges against RJ, things between them were "probably considered even now."

Even?

RJ turned and faced the back of the couch so he wouldn't have to listen to any more of the conversation. It hurt him to lie on his side, but he would rather be in a little more pain than listen to his grandpa make any more excuses for him. RJ found himself angry at him again.

It was like he couldn't make mistakes, but everybody else could. Just because the Craigs had money, they could hurt people and then buy their way out of it if there were any repercussions. RJ closed his eyes because his mind was racing and that was making his head hurt.

Then an idea hit him.

It was so simple, RJ hadn't realized it before. How could he really hurt Tim Craig? What could he do to him to make him hurt the same way that RJ did? How could RJ take away from Tim the things that he had never had? RJ's eyes opened as his mind took hold of the realization of what he was going to do. His whole body started to relax (even his mild headache began to go away), just like it always did when he started putting together a plan for revenge. The biggest difference was, this time it was going to be bigger and better than anything he had ever done. It'd be the kind of thing that would make Joel proud.

His body went cold inside with the thought.

I can do it. I'm going to enjoy doing it, he told himself.

He was going to burn down Tim Craig's house.

This would make RJ and Tim Craig really even, for everything. All those times Tim acted like he was better; all those times he held things over RJ's head ... RJ was going to finally show him that he was better than Tim ever was. He was going to show him that he could take everything away from him. He'd definitely go to juvenile hall; heck, he'd probably even go to jail at some point, but maybe that wouldn't be so bad? If he ended up where Joel had been, he'd probably be looked after. If what his grandfather said was true and Joel was no doubt headed back there, then RJ would definitely be okay. If nothing else, RJ would at least have somewhere stable to call home. The jail wasn't going anywhere and he'd just be doing time.

Later that afternoon, RJ and his grandpa were eating tuna fish sandwiches in the living room when Joel knocked on the screen door, and then walked into the house as if he still lived there. For a second, RJ had to remind himself who this was. Joel seemed a lot bigger. He was wearing jeans and a blue T-shirt, and his body was more muscular. RJ figured he'd probably been working out a lot when he'd been in jail. His brother had more tattoos on his hands and arms, and he even had one on his neck. He took all of this in at once and then let the excitement of his brother being home hit him.

"Joel!!" RJ yelled ecstatically. He got up, almost dropping his sandwich on the floor, and ran over to give his brother a hug.

"What's up, little man?" Joel asked. He gave RJ a brief hug before taking a look at him. Joel didn't seem to know exactly what he was looking for, but giving his brother a "once over" seemed like the thing to do.

"Not much. Where were you? I went to Rodney's party and everything. Where have you been?" RJ hoped he didn't sound like his mom or his grandfather asking all these questions. He was more excited to see Joel than mad. He wasn't holding a grudge for what happened with the coming home party.

"Ease up, Warden." Joel smiled squeezing RJ's shoulder. "I'd never been away that long. There were some people I needed to see."

"Might've thought to drop in to see your family instead of the no good people that helped get you sent away in the first place." RJ's grandpa's tone was harsh. He continued to eye Joel icily and he didn't seem to have the least bit of remorse (or fear) for what he'd said.

"Well, I'm here now." Joel tried to maintain an easygoing tone.

RJ was starting to get nervous. He was mad at his grandfather for getting on his brother, but he also knew that he was right and that made him even angrier.

"Now's not good enough. This kid waited for you, went to a party to meet up with you ... he was expecting you because you told him to expect you. He was expecting his big brother to be a big brother and you let him down ... again."

"Oh, you're one to talk, you drunk!" Joel's tone was as harsh as his grandpa's now. "I know all about the benders you go on. My mom told me you used to leave and not come home for days!!"

"I've made mistakes; I'm not saying I haven't," RJ's grandfather started. "But I can see you're freshly sprung, and it looks like you're already setting yourself up for a first class ticket back there."

"Look, I didn't come around to talk to you, old man! I came to see my brother and you ruined that. You think you can just come here for a month and run the place?"

"I've been here, and I'm gonna continue being here, which is more than I can say for you." RJ's grandpa had an even tone now, as if getting Joel upset was all he had wanted to do in the first place.

"Alright, RJ. I'm sorry, little bro: I'm outta here. I'll talk with you later."

And as quickly as he had returned, Joel was gone. RJ looked at his grandfather and then ran out the door after his brother. Joel was already halfway across the grass, on his way to a beat-up Oldsmobile that was running. Rodney sat in the driver's seat smoking a cigarette and listening to some hip-hop music. Joel turned around as RJ ran up to him.

"Don't leave!" RJ said. Joel stared at him, and for the first time he actually seemed to see himself in his brother.

"Hey!!" Joel started, only noticing RJ's marked face now. He put his hands on RJ's head and turned it so he could look at all the bruises. "Somebody get you?"

"Yeah," RJ said, embarrassed that he had to tell Joel that he'd lost a fight. "That guy who I beat up at the bowling alley. He got his brother on me."

Joel shook his head.

"RJ, you need me around. You don't have anybody to protect you!" He laughed.

"I don't need you to protect me," RJ stated sharply. "He's like four years older and a lot bigger."

"Still," Joel started. He looked into RJ's eyes. "I was stupid before, going away this last time. I don't wanna go back there and I won't. That old man doesn't know what he's talking about. He doesn't know me."

"He's just old and he thinks he knows everything," RJ offered.

"Well, I'm a lot smarter now. I won't get caught again."

RJ had hoped that he would say that he was never going back there because he wasn't going to get in any more trouble. He wasn't going to stop doing whatever it was he was doing; he was just going to be smarter about how he did it.

"Come on, Joel," Rodney called from the car. "You said it wasn't going to take that long."

"I'm gonna bail. I'll call you later and we'll hang out." Joel walked over and got inside Rodney's car.

RJ thought about asking "when" they were going to "hang out," but he decided not to. He knew that his brother wouldn't have an answer.

RJ walked inside and went back to the kitchen table. He put some chips in his mouth.

"What did the prodigal son have to say?" His grandpa was sipping a root beer.

"Nothing."

"I'll bet."

"WHY DO YOU HAVE TO BE SO MEAN TO HIM?!? HE JUST GOT HOME!!" RJ suddenly yelled.

"I'm sorry," His grandfather offered. He started to take a sip of his soda and then stopped. "I just think that no matter what he says, he's already committed to going down a bad road. You really have got yourself together, RJ. I'd hate to see you lose that because of someone that doesn't care about you."

"Joel cares about me."

"No, he doesn't." His grandpa's voice had no hesitation or emotion. "If you care about someone you don't just tell them you care: you show them. You may not understand this now, but when you get older, you will."

RJ was always being told that. When he got older he would understand things. Would it be like that his whole life? Would he have to wait until he was 100 to understand anything?

His grandfather continued to talk to him. He reiterated to RJ the importance of staying on the straight and narrow – how, unlike Joel, he had his whole life, his whole future ahead of him – but it didn't sound the same anymore. RJ no longer felt excited about it. The beating by Tim Craig and his brother, the way Joel had treated him, the hand he had been dealt with a dead father and sick mother: all of this made him realize he'd never really had a choice about where he was headed.

Chapter 22.

RJ was sitting in his favorite class: Computer Lab
Usually, he just played games related to Math or English, or he practiced his typing. Today, RJ had a different plan. Since he didn't have access to the internet at home, he had to use the school's connection. He had purposely sat at the one terminal that made it so his computer faced the people coming up to him. This way, if a teacher or the person who ran the computer lab came over to him, he could see them and quickly switch windows to make it look like he was doing what he should be doing. He'd also brought his notebook and a pen (something none of the other kids ever brought) so that he could write down the information he was looking for. If he was going to burn down Tim Craig's house, he would need a way to do it.

RJ got a game of Math Blaster going and as the multi-colored numbers began to move all over the screen, he clicked on the Internet Explorer logo and, after it loaded, he opened up a search page. He typed "firebombs" into the search section and pressed ENTER. A multitude of links came up, and for some reason RJ got nervous. This was something he hadn't expected. He didn't use the internet enough to know just how vague a term "firebombs" was. Just to be safe, RJ scanned the room and looked at all the kids working on the computers, talking, laughing, and hoping not to be bothered by Mrs. Perkins, the person running the lab, or Mrs. Gonzalez. Intermittently, either one of them would tell a student to "keep working" or "stop talking." Then there was the dreaded "Is that what you should be doing?"

If one of them saw what RJ was looking at at that very moment, they would definitely say that, and then it would be off to the principal's office. Since he was looking up firebombs, it would most likely only get worse.

However, none of this was scaring RJ as much as the gazillion website listings that were now displayed on his screen. His problem was he didn't know which one to pick. What if he picked the wrong one? What if he wrote down all the information and it was missing a single ingredient that might make it work? What if he went to a site that tracked terrorists and suddenly the government came after him?

RJ clicked on the first link, which brought up a simple looking site. At the top it said, "MAKING A BOMB IS EASY (AND FUN TOO)." It then listed out ingredients and it even gave RJ pictures on how he should mix the ingredients. He started taking notes as fast as he could. He had never been that great at writing, and he could barely pronounce the names of some of the things he was writing down. If he couldn't say them, how was he going to buy them? He was comforted when the site went on to say that he could pick up these things in the supermarket.

Once he got everything he needed, he quickly decided to make sure he had written it down correctly. Then, he folded up the piece of paper and, as he put it in his pocket, he clicked off the search window.

The only problem was that it wouldn't click off. An hourglass came on the screen and RJ realized that the computer had frozen.

"RJ, how are you doing over there?" Mrs. Gonzalez asked, standing a few feet in front of him.

"I'm fine," RJ stated as he discretely tried to click the screen off. RJ frantically started to press buttons, but nothing was working for him. As Mrs. Gonzalez continued to get closer, RJ felt his whole body start to get tight. It was like all of his nerves were taking over at once to punish him for what he was doing. So RJ did the only thing he could think of. The only thing he was sure would get the "MAKING A BOMB IS EASY" website off his computer screen.

He turned his system off.

It was a good move too, because right at that moment Mrs. Gonzalez came around behind him. RJ tried to restart the computer.

"Oh man!" RJ said loudly, pretending to be mad.

"Did you turn your computer off?" Mrs. Gonzalez asked. She didn't seem to suspect that RJ was doing something he shouldn't be.

"Yeah," RJ said, tapping some keys on the keyboard. He thought this might look like he was doing everything he could to bring his screen back up. "It got locked up or something. I didn't know what else to do."

"Why didn't you ask Mrs. Perkins or myself to help you out?" Mrs. Gonzalez was starting to sound annoyed.

"I don't know," RJ said. He hated saying that, but he couldn't tell Mrs. Gonzalez the truth. "I'm sorry."

Something in his eyes must've looked convincing, because a small smile emerged in the corner of her mouth.

"Next time, ask one of us for help. What do I always say? Make better choices, RJ. Now you need to reboot the whole computer. Do you know how to do that or are you starting to act stupid again?" Mrs. Gonzalez's tone was softening and RJ was so happy to hopefully be off the hook, he didn't even think about being offended by her question.

"Yeah, I think…" RJ said. Mrs. Gonzalez still helped him. She turned the computer on and navigated RJ back to the games. As she did this RJ put his hand in his pocket and touched the folded piece of paper.

He hadn't gotten caught.

RJ didn't have time to look at the list of bomb ingredients until after school. He had thought about reading it later in the school day, but the last thing he needed was for somebody to see it, ask what it was, or figure it out, and then RJ's plan would be over before he even had a chance to do it. So RJ read the list walking to the store after school.

Not only could he not pronounce the names of the things he needed, he had no idea what the names of a lot of the things were. Potassium nitrate, saltpeter... He couldn't believe that when people wanted to blow stuff up, they had to go through this much trouble finding the materials to do it. It quickly dawned on him that this wasn't the way to go. First off, RJ only had $2 on him. That wouldn't buy him much of anything. Secondly, he'd left his backpack at home, so even if he stole what he needed, RJ had nowhere to put it.

RJ put the list away and remembered something that Joel had told him. Some years ago, he and Rodney used to joke about firebombing the pizza parlor when they both got fired from it. They had been caught running a pizza scam where they took orders, they didn't ring them up in the computer, and then, since there was no record of it, they'd pocket the money. RJ had only been eight at the time, but he clearly remembered Joel and Rodney talking about burning the place down. They were going to steal a bottle of alcohol, put a rag in it, light it, and throw the bottle through the front window when the place was closed. They never did it, but RJ realized that he had a much easier solution to his problem. He stopped walking toward the supermarket and went home instead.

His firebomb had been sitting in his house the whole time.

RJ's grandpa was surprisingly not in the TV room when he walked inside.

"Grandpa?" RJ called.

No response.

He walked past the TV room and into the dining room/kitchen area.

"Hello?" There was still no response.

RJ walked into the kitchen and went over to the pantry. He had to stand on his tiptoes, but he was able to open the top door. That's when he saw them. There were two bottles up there. One was clear and the other was brown. From RJ's angle, it was difficult to see which bottle contained the most alcohol. He remained on his tiptoes and grabbed the clear bottle. He looked at it and it seemed like it was a little more than half full. Then he did the same thing with the second bottle. He decided to go with that one because it had less alcohol in it, but also because he wanted to leave his grandfather as much as he could.

RJ figured that once everything was said and done he would either be on the run somewhere or most likely in juvenile hall. If his grandpa never saw or spoke to RJ again, he might at least realize that RJ did his best to leave him as much of his alcohol as possible. He was pretty sure he was going to firebomb Tim Craig's house in the next four days. RJ took the bottle and hid it in his room. Then he went and got some old matches from a drawer in the kitchen. He hid those too.

The plan was underway.

Chapter 23.

RJ was in the TV room finishing up his homework. His grandpa sat next to him watching TV.

"You know..." his grandfather started. "I've been meaning to thank you."

"For what?" RJ asked, honestly as clueless as he sounded. Had he found out about the alcohol?

"Well, in all the commotion of your recent run-in with that Craig boy, I never got a chance to thank you for the really nice picture book."

"Oh, you're welcome," RJ said, starting to relax again.

"How'd you know I used to like taking pictures?"

"I think Mom mentioned it once. She said you used to take pictures of her when she was my age." For some reason, he hadn't thought about that at all when he bought the book.

"Yes, I did. I sure wish I still had my own camera. Heck, the thing is probably a dinosaur by today's standards. Anyway, I used to really like taking pictures. I'd go to the park, get really close to the birds, and as long as I was quiet and didn't get too close, they didn't seem to mind me too much. I used to go to the park real early in the morning, and I'd stay there until the early evening somedays."

"What happened to your camera?"

"You know, I don't know. I imagine I probably drank it away. I just remember one day I wanted to go out and shoot some pictures and it wasn't there. I've probably lost more than eighty percent of my life to alcohol. You'd be smart never to start with the stuff."

"Why don't you quit?" RJ always wondered this. It seemed like if you could start drinking something, you could just stop if you didn't want to drink it anymore.

"Well, the best way I can describe it, RJ, is that it really is a sickness. Even now, I don't drink like I did but, like breathing, I still do it. I have to ... to maintain myself. I can't help it and I can't just have one drink. But I have a limit now and I try not to cross it because that only leads to bad things. I've gone to a lot of meetings, talked with a lot of people who wanted to help me, and even when I say I'm gonna quit, I'm not gonna drink another drop ... I can't do it. I know that I won't be able to live up to that. I've got the sickness. I'm an alcoholic."

RJ thought about what his grandpa was saying. Was he destined to be that way? Would he constantly get in trouble? Deep down, RJ wondered if he really even wanted to firebomb Tim Craig's house. He didn't want to be bad ... but like his grandfather, he couldn't help it. The more he thought about it, the more RJ was starting to realize that maybe he had a sickness all his own?

The phone rang.

RJ got up, walked into the kitchen, and answered it.

"Hello?"

"Little man! What's up?" Joel asked. RJ's entire body seemed to get tense with excitement.

"Not much? Where are you?"

"I'm at Rodney's. I got nothing to do right now, I wanted to know if you wanted to hang out? We gotta do it now because I got a meeting later."

"Okay," RJ said, not caring what they were going to do.

"Alright, I'm gonna come get you. Meet me out front; I don't want to see what's-his-name or Mom." Joel laughed a little after he said that.

"Okay."

"Later."

Joel hung up the phone. RJ was so excited to hang out with his brother, he didn't want to risk telling his grandpa and having him bring him down. Instead, RJ told him he was going to Yogi's house.

"So what's going on with you?" Joel asked, staring out the window, looking at his old hometown. RJ wondered if Joel had any attachment to this place. If it bothered him at all that certain places from his past had changed. "You got a girlfriend? You married yet?"
Girlfriend? Married??
RJ knew that his big brother was only kidding around, but girls seemed to be a luxury that RJ couldn't afford. He liked plenty of girls. RJ thought there were some real cute ones at his school in fact, but he didn't think too much about asking any of them "out" or anything like that. First of all, up until a few weeks ago, the only thing on RJ's mind was if he was going to go to juvenile hall. Then before that, it always seemed like he had a fight to think about, a video game to play, or a movie to watch, and that took RJ's mind off of it. Secondly, RJ was still concerned about just surviving. He couldn't imagine somebody else not already in his family having to deal with his mom, his grandpa, and all the other things that seemed to creep up to make things less than smooth for him. Lastly, girls didn't seem to like him. Not in the way he wanted them to. They only seemed to see him as a novelty. They laughed at his jokes, but he seemed to have too much of a reputation as a troublemaker for any of them to take him seriously.

"No, not yet." RJ wished he had a different answer. He didn't think about girls too much, so all of these feelings were foreign to him. Maybe Joel could help him?

"Good," Joel laughed. "Don't get me wrong, dude: I am all about women, but they'll mess with your mind; at least they'll try, anyway. I've seen many a guy lose it over a girl … the wrong girl."

"Lose it?"

"Their soul, RJ. Their fire. A guy meets a girl, that girl usually likes the guy because they want to change him. What they end up doing is sucking the life out of him." Joel laughed again. He seemed to be in on a joke that RJ wasn't, but that was probably because he was older.

"Have you had a lot of girlfriends?" RJ realized that there was a lot about his older brother that he didn't know.

"I've had my share." Joel looked at RJ. "And I'll have many more, I'm sure. But forget getting married, having a wife, kids, a house or anything like that. All that stuff does is make you less able to do what you want."

RJ thought about what Joel had just said. He was pretty sure he understood him.

"Look at our dad," Joel continued. "Why did he have a family? Probably because Mom talked him into it. She had no idea she'd get the short end of the stick."

"But if they didn't have a family, you and I wouldn't be here," RJ stated.

"Maybe. Maybe not. Look, little bro, what are we having such a serious discussion about anyhow? What's done is done. Who cares, right? I'm just stoked to be back in town hanging with my little bro!"

What was he talking about? RJ wondered. Did he mean that things might be better if he and RJ had never been born? Even though their dad was dead, at least he had left something behind? What did Joel mean, and why did it bother RJ so much? The more he thought about it, he wasn't mad about what Joel said, but he was mad that his brother could be so wrong.

As they drove around, talking for about an hour more, RJ had a feeling that he thought about his family and his life more than Joel ever had.

Later that night, RJ was laying in his bed thinking about his plan. He decided he was going to carry it out in two days. By then it would be Friday and he figured he might have a better chance of disappearing if it was the weekend. He would get up, pack his things for school like always (and some more things, considering he was going on the run), talk to his grandfather (if he was up) while he ate breakfast, and then take the bus over to Tim Craig's house. Once he got to Tim Craig's house he would have to make sure that nobody was home. He didn't think his parents had a maid, and he was also pretty sure that both his parents worked. Once RJ knew that nobody was in the house, he would quickly run to the front of it, take the bottle of alcohol out of his backpack, light the rag that was attached to it, and throw the bottle through the window.

RJ imagined how it would look as it caught fire in the house. First, the drapes would probably burn, then the carpet, then the stairs, then all the rooms in the house.... The best moment would be when Tim's room, and everything he loved, burned up. RJ would be long gone by then. He had $89 in his drawer. He'd use that to take the bus to Fresno or San Bernardino. Once he got there, he would hide out and change his appearance. In the movies, people who went on the run did that.

RJ didn't have much of a plan beyond that. He did know that he'd probably need people who could help him. These might be street people who had been kicked around by the world just like RJ. They could show him the ropes. They'd show him how to really survive. Eventually all of these thoughts made RJ go to sleep. He knew that he'd miss his mom, Joel, his grandpa, and Yogi, but he also knew that he wouldn't have these people in his life forever anyway.

RJ Boynton had been growing up fast his whole life, but in the next 48 hours he was going to grow up a whole lot faster.

The following day at school, RJ was both out of it and more focused than ever. He'd done his homework and got his behavior contract signed (with a positive comment), but he couldn't seem to pay attention when the teachers were talking. Mrs. Gonzalez called on him two times, and one time RJ was so wrapped up in his thoughts he couldn't do anything but stare at her. The other time, RJ had sort of heard what the teacher was saying, but before he could answer the question one of the students just yelled out the answer.

RJ kept running the plan over in his head. He kept thinking about how he was going to do everything. What he was going to wear, what he was going to tell people about himself in San Bernardino (or wherever he ended up). How was he going to make his money last? It wasn't until lunch and RJ had eaten most of his food that Yogi finally said something.

"Are you okay, RJ?" Yogi asked, his lisp faint as he started to drink out of his juice box.

"Yeah," RJ said. "Why?"

"Well, you're being really quiet and you're eating almost all of your lunch."

"So?" RJ laughed, trying to seem as relaxed as normal. He wanted to tell Yogi about his plan, but he couldn't. It wasn't that he didn't trust him, but that wasn't a secret he felt like laying on him. It would probably be more of a burden than anything else.

"You just don't usually eat that much."

"I didn't have breakfast. I stayed up late last night playing video games so I missed it."

"I went online and got a bunch of codes for the next time we play at your house," Yogi offered.

"I don't like using those. I think it makes the game too easy."

"Not if you suck at it like me." Yogi took a bite of his sandwich.

RJ and Yogi continued talking; then they walked around the school and talked about going to the movies that weekend. Then they went back to class. Before RJ knew it, the school day was over.

The sun was shining bright as RJ walked home. He looked around at the neighborhood he'd lived in his whole life and he started to wonder where his new home would be and what it might be like. Would he even have a new neighborhood? Would he end up in juvenile hall and then eventually jail? What would people in Bentonville say about him?

He imagined it would be something like, "He'd always been a bad kid. It wasn't surprising that he burned the Craig house down because RJ Boynton had never been any good anyway." Would anybody besides his grandfather remember the few months before RJ did what he was going to do that he had tried to turn himself around?

One thing was sure: after tomorrow, Joel wouldn't be the only legend in the neighborhood. RJ had always been in his brother's shadow. He'd always been overlooked because Joel was seen as such a leader and a tough guy. RJ was about to change all that. People would have to recognize who he was ... even if it was for all the wrong reasons.

Chapter 24.

That Thursday night, RJ went to bed early. He thought he might have trouble sleeping, so he lay down around 8:30 and, surprisingly, went right to sleep. He got up at 6:30, ate some cereal, and took one final look around his house. He was having trouble because he wanted to be invisible, but his house was small, and his grandpa was sleeping in the living room. He knew that if he stood in there looking around, taking one last look at things, his presence would probably be enough to wake him up. Still, he was sad that he wasn't going to have one last conversation with him.

RJ looked at the few pictures of his family that hung in the hallway. In them were his mom, his dad, Joel and RJ when he was a baby.

Had time gone that quickly? he wondered. Had he been a baby one day and then a 13 year-old with all these problems the next?

He looked at a picture of him and Joel in the park when they were younger, and he wondered how someone became the person they are. He stared at a picture of his mom when she was younger – before she'd gotten sick – and she was smiling.

RJ moved throughout the house thinking of everything he'd done there. He walked through the living room, the tiny dining room, the kitchen, etc. RJ thought about when he was a real little boy all the way to that very moment. It was like watching a movie of his life at warp speed. He had lived his whole life in this house, and in less than one hour he'd probably never see it again.

He quickly blocked these thoughts from his mind and walked back to his bedroom. RJ Boynton had work to do. No more letting people make up their minds about who he was.

RJ took one last look at his grandpa and then quietly shut the door to his house. He walked across the front lawn to the sidewalk. He thought about turning around to give his house one last look, but he figured he'd better not. Somebody might see him and wonder what he was doing. Also, the longer he stayed in one place, the more that gave somebody a chance to talk to him. RJ knew that time was everything. The longer he waited, the longer he might get distracted, his plans might get altered, he might think twice about what he was doing...

He kept telling himself that he didn't want to hurt anybody. RJ just wanted to take something from Tim Craig. To show him that he could really hurt Tim the way that his words had hurt RJ. That was all.

RJ's backpack was really light today. He'd considered bringing some books in case he needed to open his backpack (he could hide the taped bottle behind them) in front of anyone, but he figured he was fine how he was. He just had his makeshift bomb and some clothes.

RJ had even thought about leaving a note for his grandpa and his mom, but he couldn't think about what to write. He also didn't want to say goodbye, because he didn't not want to see his family again. He had thought about apologizing in advance for what he was about to do, but he didn't know how. RJ was only used to saying sorry after he had a reason to be sorry for something.

Cars passed RJ as he made his way down the street.

Nobody has any idea what I'm about to do, he thought. That was the part of his plan that excited him. The Craig household was probably having a normal day, but in the next hour their lives would be interrupted like they had never been before.

All RJ had ever wanted was to matter to somebody. Until his grandpa came into his life, he had never known what that felt like. He didn't want to let him down, to make all those

talks about doing the right thing and staying on the right path seem wasted, but RJ couldn't help it. Those were just words. He had tried doing what his grandfather said and he'd gotten beaten up. If he didn't stand up now, the Tim Craigs of the world would always hurt people like RJ ... unless the people like RJ hurt them. Bad.
    Then he could win.

    RJ had been in such deep thought as he made his way to the bus stop, he only noticed Rodney's car when it made a U-turn. It pulled up next to him. Joel was sitting shotgun and Rodney was driving.
    "Need a ride, little man?" Joel asked.
    Sometimes it bothered RJ when people called him that, but never when Joel did it.
    "No," RJ said. Normally, he'd have jumped at the chance to have everybody see him pull into school with Joel and his friends. It'd be great. They'd roll up, blasting music, and the teachers and all the students would just stare in amazement as RJ stepped out and walked onto the campus. Everybody would see who he was with, and nobody would give RJ a second look for fear of what the retaliation might be. "I'm almost at school."
    "So what? How often do I get to give my kid brother a ride to school?" Joel looked half shocked that RJ wasn't already in the car.
    "You don't have to, okay?"
    "No, it's not okay."
    RJ started to move away, but Joel got out of the moving car and grabbed him before he could get any further.
    "What's your problem, kid?" Joel asked angrily.
    There was no way he could get away, and the last thing he needed this morning was to have a fistfight with his brother. If

he didn't tell Joel his plan, they were going to take him to school.

Or, maybe they wouldn't?

The big problem was that if RJ didn't do it today – if he didn't follow through with firebombing Tim Craig's house – he might never get up the nerve to do it again. There was no other way. He'd have to tell Rodney and Joel why he wanted to be left alone that morning.

RJ sat in the backseat of the car as Joel and Rodney stared at him. Rodney had pulled it into the parking lot of a supermarket. Joel was holding his backpack. It was open. After telling them about his plan, he showed them his makeshift firebomb just to prove that he wasn't lying.

As RJ told the story and his reasons for wanting to do this, a weird expression came to Joel's face. He was actually listening to RJ. All their lives, Joel had dispensed advice and RJ had listened to him and asked questions. Then he went away and RJ had tried to use his logic to form some sort of code to live by. He'd done okay with it but he hadn't really done anything other than come off like a pint-size, carbon copy of his brother. Now, as RJ talked to the person who had helped shape his value system and thought process, he could see that his big brother was proud.

"Remember what I said last time I saw you?" Joel asked.

"Not really," RJ said.

"You need me around. What you're talking about doing is big time. There's no way I can let my little brother walk into something like that alone. No way. He's got too much to lose, right Rodney?"

"Yup." Rodney took out a cigarette and lit it.

"So tell us how to get to this guy's house. You'll get away clean. You won't even need to go on the run."

RJ liked that idea. He wouldn't have to leave his grandpa or his mom. Maybe Joel ... he'd be so impressed with what RJ did, maybe he might stick around too? He suddenly felt a wave of relief rush over him.

It wouldn't last.

Rodney drove past Tim Craig's house two times before parking a few blocks away.

"Alright," Joel started. "We've gotta make this quick. We hang out here too long, somebody in this neighborhood is gonna call the cops."

RJ had never done anything like this with Joel. He was getting an education today. He always wondered how these things worked, but he figured that Joel knew what he was doing. Joel had something special that made people listen to him.

"So what do you think?" Rodney asked.

"Well, the way I see it…" Joel eyed RJ. "There's nobody home, right?"

"I don't think so."

"If we go around back, there should be a sliding door. I'm sure I can work it," Joel stated.

Sliding door? RJ asked himself. Was Joel thinking about going inside the house and firebombing it from the inside? Maybe that would make it harder to figure out who did it?

"Are you gonna put the stuff in the backpack?" Rodney and Joel seemed to be having a conversation between themselves that RJ wasn't a part of.

"You got your piece, right?"

Rodney nodded slightly and then pointed at the glove compartment. Joel opened it up and took out a gun. It looked smaller than RJ thought it would (he had only really seen guns in movies before), and it was a lot darker, too. Joel held it low and made sure it was loaded.

"Why do you need that?" RJ's voice was starting to shake.

"Kid, this is perfect," Joel started. "If you firebomb the place, they'll know it was you. You got a beef with this family. This way, Rodney and I go in, we take some stuff of theirs, real valuable stuff, we'll drop you off at school after. Nobody will suspect you had anything to do with it."

"Won't they wonder why I was late?" RJ was doing his best to wrap his mind around this idea. He had wanted to destroy the Craig house, but now Joel was complicating his plan. Taking away RJ's idea because he was stupid and Joel was smart.

"No, because I'm gonna forge a note from Mom. We're gonna drop you off near the school so nobody sees our car. Even if they think it was you and they start asking questions, Mom's cool: she's not gonna narc you out. You're as free as a bird. And the best thing is, you're the point man on this job: you see any cops or anything, you just honk the horn. Rodney and I are gonna kick you some cash after we sell the stuff." Joel seemed to be making all of this up as he went along. RJ's plan had been simple, but he thought about it for a long time before he started putting it in motion. Joel had made this all up on the spot and there was no talking him out of it. "Hold this."

Joel gave RJ his homemade firebomb, which he almost dropped.

"Are we ready to do it?" Rodney asked. RJ always thought of him as Joel's sidekick. Somebody who hung on his every word before he waited to move. He was realizing that, as soon as things started to get serious, as soon as business was about to happen, Rodney became more assertive and was ready to do anything Joel needed done. RJ was amazed at how one minute they could be driving down the street and then, the minute action presented itself, these two guys could instantly become criminals. Maybe they were so steeped in this way of life that that's what made it so easy for them to act this way? Maybe RJ would eventually become like this?

RJ found himself going along with everything. If he had been on his own, he most likely would have done the job by now. RJ was working with Rodney and Joel now ... just like he'd always wanted.

"People like this, RJ, you firebomb their home, it doesn't mean anything. They have insurance and they'll get even more money! But you steal from them, like they steal from you when they insult you or put you down, they can't replace some of the stuff they've got inside their home. It's got a value that's more than money. They may be insured, but they'll never get back what they had exactly. That's how you hurt these kinds of people, RJ."

Rodney pulled up to Tim Craig's perfect house, and in the front window RJ vaguely saw someone. Then he noticed a small car out front with a placard on both sides that said, "Anita's Cleaning Service" and a telephone number. A cleaning person must've arrived while they were talking a few blocks away.

"You can't do it," RJ said.

"What?" Rodney asked. Joel glared at him.

"Their cleaning person is here."

Rodney looked at Joel. Joel looked at the house.

"Who cares? She'll never know we were in the house."

"How?" RJ asked.

"Because she won't!" Joel yelled.

"You can't do it!" RJ grabbed his brother's arm.

"Don't grab me!" Joel started punching RJ on the top of the head. "You just do what I tell you or we'll beat your ass and leave you here!! Everyone will know what a wuss RJ really is!!

Two minutes!! That's all we'll need!! Things get suspicious, honk the horn twice!"

Joel stopped hitting him. RJ glared at his brother.

The coolest person in town.

The neighborhood legend.

Tim Craig and his brother may have done a number on him when they jumped RJ, but he felt one hundred times worse now.

"I thought you didn't want to go back to jail?!?!" RJ cried. Tears were coming to his eyes. The last thing he wanted to do was cry in front of Joel and Rodney, but he couldn't help it.

"What?!?" Joel was getting even madder, and he hit RJ again. "We're gonna have a talk about your mouth, kid! You just do what we need you to do or we'll kill you!! Brother or no brother. I mean it: I'll kill you, RJ."

Joel turned, and he and Rodney got out of the car. RJ lay there and cried for a moment, but he quickly stopped. He couldn't cry now ... he couldn't try and understand why he didn't have the family unit everyone else seemed to have. Why nobody other than his grandpa (and his mom sometimes) seemed to care about what happened to him. He couldn't think about any of this ... he had to act. He had to do something.

An idea came to RJ. It wasn't the smartest thing he could do, and it wouldn't solve all his problems, but it would solve this problem.

For now...

RJ grabbed the firebomb and got out of the car. He quickly took out some matches from his pocket, lit them (thankfully, they still worked), then he touched the flame to the old rag that was connected to the bottle. He dropped the bottle into Rodney's car and ran away as small flames and smoke spread throughout the vehicle.

A few minutes later, as RJ was running past a gas station, he called 911 and told them there was a burning car in front of Tim Craig's house. After that, RJ kept running until he came to the Family Four movie theater. Since summer was almost here, the first show was at 9:30am. RJ was 25 minutes early. He didn't know what movie he paid to see, and if he'd thought about it, he would've been more worried that the person who sold him his ticket would question why he wasn't in school. RJ didn't think about any of that. He was just happy to be somewhere that nobody could see him for awhile.

Chapter 25.

RJ stayed in the movies all day. It wasn't until he went to the bathroom between shows that he realized that it was early evening, and he probably should go home.
 Go home?
 Go home?????
 RJ wasn't sure that he had anything to go home to. What if Joel and Rodney had robbed the house, put out the fire in Rodney's car, and then got away? What if the fire from the car had spread to Tim Craig's house and then set the whole neighborhood on fire? What if people had been hurt, or worse, killed by what RJ had done?
 RJ's mind slowly turned back to Joel...
 His grandpa had been right. He was no good. He may have been RJ's brother – his blood – but that didn't matter. Joel didn't care about RJ or anyone else. He was a scam artist. A thief. Everything you wouldn't ever want in your life. RJ had looked up to him. He had worshipped Joel. Everyone did. RJ felt special because being Joel Boynton's little brother made him feel special. It was yet another piece of RJ's puzzle of normalcy that was gone. Normally, this would've bothered him, especially since having a normal family life was all RJ thought he wanted. But now, he wanted something even more, regardless of what awaited him when he got home ... he didn't want anything to do with Joel or that life. Ever.
 RJ was gonna walk the straight and narrow again. Not for his grandpa or his mom ... but for himself.
 He had thought that if he hurt Tim Craig's family, that somehow it might make up for the family unit that RJ had been denied his whole life. That somehow he could gain something from Tim Craig's loss. RJ had finally realized that, even when

you hurt people – when you take things from them, just because you've had things taken from you – you both lose.
RJ Boynton had been fighting the world since he was born. It pushed him, so he pushed back. He figured he'd be fighting it in some way all his life. However, for the first time, his anger was finally directed at the one person that could actually help make a difference. At the person who had some control over it ... himself.
RJ rounded the corner of his block and didn't change his pace at all when he saw the two police cars out front.

Joel and Rodney had both been arrested. Apparently, they had robbed the house (the cleaning lady had hid in a closet and called 911 on her cell phone) and then come outside to find their car in flames. At that time, both the police and the fire trucks pulled up. It didn't take Joel and Rodney long to sell RJ out and tell the police about the firebomb. Later, when RJ spoke to the police, he told them everything he could about his involvement in the crime. Due to RJ's age, the police only brought him down to the station for questioning. This would be one more thing on his record, but since he had helped stop the crime, and he did alert the police to the burning car, RJ wasn't going to be charged. Amazingly, he had dodged another bullet.

Chapter 26.

When RJ was absent the first couple of days of the week, Principal Jennings had probably told the school not to bring up what had happened between RJ and the Craig family. Again. RJ hadn't felt like going to school that Monday. Tuesday he had to go down to the police station and answer a bunch more questions. This probably accounted for why nobody brought up what had happened when he returned Wednesday. Unlike when he'd run through the glass door at the bowling alley, no kids even brought it up at lunch. He told Yogi all about what had happened, but even as RJ was telling the story to a willing audience, he realized that what happened that Friday didn't need to be discussed. RJ was ashamed of the fact that the plan had gone that far to begin with.

At the end of the day, as he got up to leave Mrs. Gonzalez's class, RJ just happened to be the last kid out of the room. Things had been business as usual in her room. The biggest surprise was that RJ didn't have to make up any of the homework he'd missed.

"I'm proud of you, RJ," Mrs. Gonzalez said. She smiled at him, but not in a joking way. "You made a good choice."

"Thanks, Mrs. Gonzalez," RJ said. He smiled, but not that much. The event was still too fresh in his mind.

"Yeah, you made a good choice." Mrs. Gonzalez continued to smile. "Finally."

RJ smiled a little more. When he looked into her eyes, he could tell that she meant what she was saying. He walked out of her classroom.

Chapter 27.

Joel and Rodney were both sent to jail. Eventually, they would be shipped off to a state prison for a very long time. RJ sat in court during the arraignment with his grandfather and his crying mother. Joel didn't even look at them.

"Nobody wants to go back here..." Joel started. "It just happens. It's gonna be a lot different from where I'm going."

RJ and Joel were sitting across from each other in the contact room of Rittner Jail. The room felt really old to RJ. The paint on the walls was faded. The tables looked old. The chairs were old. It looked like a place that time had forgotten. There were some other people in the room talking as three armed guards kept their eyes on everyone. RJ had expected to feel really nervous here, but for some reason he didn't. He had been more nervous on the long bus ride up with his grandpa than he was when he actually got in the facility. That was probably because he could leave. Also, having guards nearby in case Joel got really mad at him again was also reassuring.

"I wish you weren't in here," RJ offered. Even though he wasn't nervous, he was having trouble thinking of things to talk about. He didn't think Joel would ever speak to him again, so it was a shock when he called the house and asked RJ to come up for a visit. "I didn't think you'd ever want to see me again."

"I didn't think you'd ever want to see me, either," Joel said. He sounded apologetic. RJ didn't know his brother that well, but apologetic probably wasn't something he sounded like much.

"I didn't know what to do at the house ... but I'm glad I didn't do what I was originally planning."

"Yeah," Joel laughed. "You were out of your league with that plan. It took guts to try, though. Especially at your age. You're a tough kid, RJ ... but not the kind of tough for a place like this."

Normally, RJ might have felt insulted by someone saying that (even Joel), but he knew it was the truth. He was happy that he didn't belong in jail.

"I know that now," RJ offered.

"Good. This place sucks." Joel stared at his little brother. RJ used to want to be like Joel so badly that he'd even wanted to look like him. Now he knew that things like that didn't matter as much. "I could tell you that I learned something, but I'd be lying. When I get out ... it'll probably only be a matter of time before I'm coming back again."

For some reason, RJ started remembering what Joel said about their father. About how maybe his dad's life would've been better if he hadn't gotten married and had kids.

"You're wrong about Dad, you know," RJ said. Even though he didn't look at Joel in the same way anymore, RJ felt a tinge of fear in the way Joel looked at him after he said that.

"What about Dad?" Joel asked sternly. "Dad's dead."

"I think he was glad that he had a family. It's good that we're here ... even if we mess up sometimes."

"Maybe I am wrong..." Joel started, the stern expression still on his face. "All I know is that a dad that cares about his family doesn't go getting himself killed in a junkie hotel room."

"What about a big brother who keeps getting himself in trouble?"

RJ met his brother's gaze. The way Joel stared back at him seemed to show that he was actually seeing RJ as a person, and not just as a miniature version of him.

One of the guards walked over and stood about two feet behind Joel.

"Five minutes," the guard stated. Then he walked away.

RJ and Joel continued to stare at one another.

"Thanks for coming to see me," Joel said.

"Okay," RJ said, nodding his head.

"Tell Mom I said, 'Hi.'" Joel stood up. "I'll call you or something in a couple of weeks."

Joel walked away, leaving RJ alone again.

As he rode the bus home with his grandpa, they didn't talk much. His grandfather didn't ask him any questions about his brother. RJ didn't mind either. After all his little brother admiration, he knew he'd probably never see his legendary brother again. They might talk if they crossed paths somehow, but RJ didn't really care either way. Instead of always longing for the family he didn't have, RJ was going to be just fine with the family he did.

Chapter 28.

Summer was upon the Boynton home, and at his grandpa's request, RJ had started reading a little more instead of only playing video games. In spite of everything that had happened, RJ had had the best academic school year since his father died when he was eight. Mrs. Gonzalez was practically crying when she told RJ how good he had done that semester. He'd gotten B's in all of his subjects. With some pride, he also declared that he was going to do better next year when he got into eighth grade. Mrs. Gonzalez told him that she looked forward to seeing it.

He'd also given his mom the remainder of the money he'd saved up. It wasn't much, but it was something. RJ had also gone down to Lincoln Lanes with his grandpa and worked out a deal where he was going to volunteer his time – three days a week, two hours a day – so that he could pay off the remainder of the bill from the damage he'd caused. He wasn't happy to have to work over the summer, but he was helping his family, so he didn't feel too bad.

RJ had also been trying to spend a lot of time with Yogi, as he was going to be moving. His dad's new job was going to be taking Yogi and his family to New Jersey. RJ was really going to miss Yogi. He had been the best friend he'd ever had, but he also understood, or at least was beginning to understand, that this was the way things went sometimes.

The world wasn't against RJ Boynton. He wasn't the only person who had had problems. He still got mad about things, and if the right situation came up, his temper could flare up like always, but he seemed to have come to an understanding with himself. He found that he was just trying to enjoy the people in his life and not worry so much about everything now. RJ no longer felt like he needed to look over his shoulder in anticipation of what might happen. He was still scared, but he was doing his best to manage that by facing up to it instead of fighting it.

After Joel was sentenced (he got 10 years in prison), RJ found himself checking the mail sometimes to see if his brother had written him. After a few weeks of that, RJ stopped. He also was still nervous that Rodney might send somebody after him. Eventually, RJ gave up worrying about that too. If somebody came after him, they came after him. If Joel and Rodney waited until they got out of jail to deal with him, they would be much older and so would RJ. He'd be able to deal with them better then. At least he hoped he would be. Who knows? By that time, RJ figured he might not even be living in that neighborhood. Maybe he would be in college? He might have a good job somewhere? In another state? His job might be so good he could move his mom and grandfather too?

These were the things RJ was thinking about now.

RJ figured it was time he fixed up the dead looking grass in front of the house. With his grandpa's help, they got the lawn mower out of the garage and RJ went to work. He was mowing the lawn when a letter from the Bentonville School District came. The letter was addressed to his mom, but she was working. This was a letter she had been getting about RJ for the past six years since he started taking "special classes." It marked his progress for the year and also gave an indication of the classes RJ would be in the following year. He had never cared about it because it always said that he was going to stay in "special education." For some reason, after everything that had happened this year, he thought it might actually say something different. RJ brought it out to his grandpa, who was on his knees in front of the house pulling weeds.

"This came," RJ said, showing his grandpa the letter.

His grandpa stopped working, wiped his brow, and took it out of RJ's hand.

"It's addressed to your mom." He handed the letter back to RJ.

"But it's about me ... I think it might be good," RJ offered. He had never wanted to open a letter this much in his life. Not even one from Joel.

"You know that opening mail that isn't yours is a federal offense?"

"What's a federal offense?"

"It means don't open it."

RJ stared at his grandpa, knowing he was right, but also knowing that he didn't want to wait until his mom got home so he could find out his academic fate for the eighth grade.

His grandfather smiled at him.

"It better be good."

RJ smiled, ripped open the letter, and started to read it.

Dear Miss Boynton,

In light of Russell's major improvements in the past year, we are considering the possibility that, if this improvement continues, we will place Russell in general education courses in reading and math for the spring term of his eighth grade year. Should his improvement continue, Russell could be in general education with resource support for all of his courses going forward into the fall of the ninth grade school year...

There was some more to the letter, but RJ had read all that he needed to read. He didn't jump for joy; he didn't even yell out in excitement; he just smiled and explained it to his grandfather the best he could. RJ might finally be getting an opportunity to show everyone what he was capable of. He knew that he had to keep working hard, and if he did that, he'd have to work even harder to show people that he belonged in all general education classes. RJ would probably be scrutinized a lot more than most of the students, but after so many years of being written off as a troublemaker, he wasn't going to mind a little positive attention.

His grandpa was so happy, he told RJ that work was done for the day, and they went out to lunch.

As they sat on the bus staring out the window, RJ thought about the first bus ride he and his grandpa had taken together. He had seemed so different then, and it had only been six months ago.

"You watch kid," his grandfather said with a smile. "You keep working the way you're working and everything is going to be fine. You'll do things and go places you never dreamed you could go."

"Yeah, I hope so," RJ said, as if he was realizing for the first time that his life could actually have a future. A real future.

"You will … you just need to keep doing what you're doing. Even when it's tough and it doesn't seem like all that hard work is getting you anywhere. There's no easy road. What doesn't get you anywhere is taking up with the wrong people. Don't be so quick to try and fit in; just be yourself."

"How do you know who the bad people are? Sometimes you think people care about you and then you realize they don't."

"Well, this isn't a foolproof solution, but remember how Joel made you feel?"

"Yeah."

"Well, you find yourself hanging around with people that make you feel that way, then you know you've got the wrong kind of friends."

"But what about someone like Tim Craig? He comes from a good home. He's rich…"

"Money isn't everything," his grandpa interrupted. "It also shows you that someone can have all the advantages in the world and still end up rotten. Think about that good, because you'll never backslide thinking you've got an excuse."

"Yeah," RJ said.

The bus came to a stop, but RJ and his grandpa still had a few more stops before they got to the Oak Pine Diner. His grandfather even said that if there was time, they might even try and go to the movies.

RJ listened to him as they talked, but he also noticed that his grandpa seemed to listen to him more. His grandfather's advice sounded better again, too. Like it did when RJ first heard it. It was as if the things he talked about – RJ making something of himself if he worked hard – could really happen now. And those things would happen … as long as RJ wanted them to.

The End

About the Author

Evan Jacobs was born in Long Island, New York and he moved to to Irvine, California when he was 4 years old. He lived there for a year before relocating with his family to Fountain Valley, where he still lives. As a filmmaker, Evan has directed 10 low budget films and he's also had various screenplays produced and realized by other directors. He is currently hard at work on several movie and book projects. Evan also works for the Tustin Unified School District as a Behavior Interventionist in their Special Education department. JD is his second young adult novel. You can find out more about him at www.anhedeniafilms.com.

Made in the USA
Charleston, SC
29 October 2011